FOXES ON THE FARM

'Mandy!' James shouted urgently, stopping his bike and leaning on the handlebars. 'I've just thought of something awful,' he said ominously.

'What?' Mandy called, slamming on her brakes. She backed up quickly at the sight of James's worried face. 'James, what is it? Tell me!'

'We were so pleased to see that fox, that we didn't notice at the time,' James said.

'Notice what?' Mandy asked, anxiously.

'Don't you realise where that fox must have come from?' James said softly, staring at Mandy as he waited for realisation to dawn on her.

Mandy thought. Next to the Riddings' land was . . . 'Oh no, James! It came from the direction of Upper Welford Hall,' she said in a faint voice.

James nodded. 'Sam Western's place,' he groaned. 'We know how much *he* cares about wildlife. He and Dennis Skinner will shoot anything that moves.'

Mandy nodded grimly. She and James had already had several run-ins with Sam Western and his gamekeeper Dennis Skinner. The two men had poisoned one of Lydia Fawcett's goats and had been responsible for setting the traps that had nearly killed Lucky and his mother.

'If Sam Western found foxes on his land,' James voiced her thoughts, 'he'd be sure to want to start a foxhunt again.'

Animal Ark series

LUCY DANIELS

Foxes
— *on the* —
Farm

Illustrations by Ann Baum

h
*Hodder
Children's
Books*

a division of Hodder Headline Limited

Special thanks to Tanis Jordan
Thanks also to C. J. Hall, B.Vet.Med., M.R.C.V.S., for reviewing
the veterinary information contained in this book.

Animal Ark is a trademark of Working Partners Limited
Text copyright © 1999 Working Partners Limited
Created by Working Partners Limited, London W6 0QT
Original series created by Ben M. Baglio
Illustrations copyright © 1999 Ann Baum

First published in Great Britain in 1999 within *Wildlife Ways*
by Hodder Children's Books

This single volume edition 2000

A Catalogue record for this book is available from the British Library

ISBN 0 340 73663 1

Typeset by Avon Dataset Ltd, Bidford-on-Avon, Warks

Printed and bound in Great Britain by
Clays Ltd, St Ives plc

Hodder Children's Books
a division of Hodder Headline Limited
338 Euston Road
London NW1 3BH

One

Mandy Hope saw the note as soon as she came in through the door. It was propped against a bowl of daffodils on the kitchen table. 'Ring Michelle Holmes,' she read out loud. Her mother had jotted down the number and added 'URGENT!!' to the bottom of the note.

Mandy frowned. Dumping her schoolbag on a chair, she reached for the phone. Why was Michelle ringing her? Michelle Holmes was the presenter of the radio programme *Wildlife Ways*. She had made a programme about the hedgehog refuge that Mandy and her best friend James Hunter had helped to set up, and had even supplied them with radio tags for the young hedgehogs so they could keep track of them when they left the nest. Mandy hurriedly punched in the numbers. Michelle answered on the third ring.

'Michelle, it's Mandy Hope. Mum left a note to ring you urgently,' Mandy said.

'Oh, hi, Mandy. Thanks for getting back to me so quickly. I've got wonderful news. *Wildlife Ways* is being turned into a TV show! I wondered if you'd like to help at all . . .'

'Would I like to? I'd *love* to!' Mandy exclaimed.

Michelle laughed and went on, enthusiastically filling Mandy in on her plans. Mandy listened with mounting excitement. 'So, Mandy, I need to start as soon as possible. It will be great to have you and James to help,' she finished. 'Speak to your parents and, if it's OK, I'll see you later, at about six-thirty. Oh, just one more thing, Mandy . . .' Michelle hesitated, '. . . we need to start filming in a few days' time to make our deadline. So it's quite tight.'

'That's OK,' Mandy replied. 'We broke up for a week's holiday today. Wait till I tell James about this!' James Hunter was Mandy's best friend. He was a year younger than her, and almost as keen on animals as she was. 'Bye,

Michelle,' Mandy put down the phone. '*Yes!*' she said with a big grin on her face. She couldn't believe it!

Mandy dashed through the door connecting the old stone cottage where the Hopes lived to the modern vet's surgery at the back where Mandy's parents had their practice. She arrived in the waiting-room, still clutching her mum's note in her hand.

'Where's the fire?' Jean Knox the receptionist asked, removing her glasses and giving Mandy a startled look.

'Sorry,' Mandy gasped. 'It's just that I've got *such* exciting news and I can't *wait* to tell Mum and Dad.'

'Well, you'd better go through to the surgery,' Jean said, smiling. 'Your father's scrubbing up. He's got one more operation to do this afternoon and Simon's assisting him. I think your mum's in with them too.'

Mandy spun round and pushed through the surgery door. Jean followed her.

'Mum, Dad, guess what!' Mandy stood dramatically in the middle of the room, beaming broadly.

Adam Hope was leaning over the sink rinsing the soap bubbles from his hands. 'School's finished for the holidays?' he called over his shoulder.

'Much better than that!' Mandy was enjoying this. 'Fantastic, in fact!'

'Might it be anything to do with a telephone message?' asked Mandy's mum, who was sorting through some files.

Simon, the practice nurse, grinned at Mandy as he took a new pair of thin rubber gloves from the cupboard and began to unwrap them ready for Mr Hope to put on.

'You all know already!' Mandy said, pretending to be upset.

'*I* don't. Nobody tells me anything,' Adam Hope said, drying his hands. 'Simon mentioned to us that Michelle had an idea, and Mum spoke to her earlier, but *I'm* still in the dark.' He dropped the paper towels into the bin.

'Well,' Mandy began, trying to control her excitement, 'Michelle is making a *Wildlife Ways* TV programme and she wants to know if James and I want to get involved. She wants to make a film about foxes first, and we're going to help collect information about where they live and what they do.' The words all tumbled out at once. 'She wants to come here to tell us all about it after work tonight. Isn't that brilliant?'

'How exciting,' said Jean from the doorway. 'Our very own TV researcher!'

Mandy turned to face her, pretending to be haughty. 'One day, Jean, you might *beg* for my autograph.' Everyone laughed and then Mandy continued. 'Michelle is making three programmes to begin with. And if they're a success she gets to make a whole series! Isn't it great?'

Simon looked up from preparing the surgical instruments for the operation. 'I told Michelle a while ago that you found a vixen who'd given birth while caught in a trap.' He wheeled over the anaesthetic apparatus. 'She was very impressed that you'd rescued the newborn cub and his mother.'

Mandy felt a glow of satisfaction as she remembered how they had managed to free the vixen from the deadly trap and save her life. Mandy had named the cub Lucky, as he was the only one of four cubs to survive.

'Hey, wouldn't it be good if we spotted them? Lucky and his mum, I mean.' Mandy was delighted to think she might see the cub again. 'I wonder if they're still on their old territory. Do you think Lucky would remember me?'

'I'm sure he might, it wasn't *that* long ago, Mandy,' her mum replied. 'But you mustn't encourage him to make contact with you,' she reminded her, taking off her white coat and hanging it up. 'His best chance of survival is to stay wild.'

'When are you going to tell James the good news?' asked Mr Hope.

'Right now!' Mandy decided. 'Then I can be back in time to do all my jobs.'

'He's a member of the Welford Wildlife Watchers, isn't he?' her dad asked. 'That might come in handy.'

'Yep. James is really good at spotting tracks,' Mandy agreed. She would have liked to join the group herself but now she was twelve she had started helping out at Animal Ark and she didn't have the time.

'I'll do your jobs tonight,' Simon offered.

'Oh thanks, Simon,' Mandy said gratefully. She turned to her mum and dad. 'Is that OK?' Mandy asked them. She loved helping out in her parents' surgery but right now her head was full of foxes and she was dying to tell James the good news.

'Yes, go on love, we'll let you off this once,' Adam Hope agreed, holding out his arms as

Simon put an operating gown on him and tied it at the back.

'Thanks, Dad!' Mandy said, heading for the door.

Adam Hope called her back. 'I know you – you'll probably start looking for foxes before you've even met up with Michelle, but remember to ask permission if you want to search on people's land,' he warned her. 'Some farmers can be very particular about trespassers!'

Mandy grimaced. 'If you mean Sam Western, I don't think we'll be looking on *his* land. We all know he hates foxes.' Sam Western was a ruthless local farmer who wanted to start up a foxhunt and rid the area of foxes.

'See you later, everyone,' Mandy said, halfway out of the door.

'Don't forget to change your clothes first!' Emily Hope called after her.

Mandy was already on her way upstairs. She changed into a comfortable blue tracksuit and set off. As she cycled to James's house she racked her brains for a plan. They would have to check every woodland and spinney in the area and do some trekking on the moor as well. James was sure to come up with some good ideas.

Mrs Hunter was weeding the front garden when Mandy arrived. 'Hello, there. James is in the back garden with Blackie,' she said, smiling. 'He's mending his bike; he got a puncture turning into the drive this evening.'

Mandy walked around the house and looked out over the lawn. James had his bike upside-down by the beech tree and was just levering the tyre back on to its wheel. 'Hi,' he called. James's black Labrador spotted Mandy and bounded towards her.

'Whoa, Blackie! Down!' Mandy laughed, as the dog jumped up and tried to lick her face. 'I know you're always pleased to see me.' She kneeled down near James and rubbed Blackie's ears. He loved the attention and rolled over, thumping his tail on the ground.

'Listen, James, I've got some fantastic news!' Mandy sat back on her heels impatiently, waiting for his full attention.

Hearing the excitement in Mandy's voice, James stopped pumping up the tyre and looked at her.

'Are you ready for this?' Mandy asked. She took a deep breath. 'Michelle Holmes wants us to help with a television programme about foxes.'

For a while, James just stared at Mandy. Then,

as the news sank in, he leaped to his feet
sending the pump flying. Blackie sprang up
with an excited bark and made a grab for it.
'No you don't!' James got there first. 'That's
fantastic! Us, helping with a TV programme!
Wow! When do we start?'

'As soon as possible!' Mandy told him,
jumping up. 'Let's go to The Riddings. We can
ask the Spry sisters' permission to start our
search on their land first thing in the morning,'
she said excitedly.

James righted his bike and tested the tyre. 'I
should take Blackie for a walk first, he's been
waiting for it,' he said.

'We could take him with us,' Mandy suggested.
James nodded, and fetched Blackie's lead.

Soon they were cycling slowly down the lane
so that Blackie could trot beside them. There
was a gentle breeze and the last of the blossom
fluttered from the trees. The early summer
sunshine was warm as they rode along.

'Walter Pickard showed me how to look for
foxes once, when we were on a badger watch,'
James called out to Mandy, who was riding in
front. Walter Pickard was the secretary of the
Welford Wildlife Watchers. 'We could ask him
for some advice.'

'Can't hear you!' Mandy slowed down so James could catch up.

'I said, Walter must know more about the countryside than almost anybody,' James told her, keeping close to the side so Blackie could run along the grassy bank.

'That's a point,' Mandy said. She pushed a wayward strand of her fair hair behind her ears. 'You're right – he's the perfect person to ask.'

Mandy and James pedalled up the Walton road towards The Riddings, where the Spry sisters lived. From the crest of the hill they freewheeled down until they reached the bridge over the stream, where Mandy stopped so suddenly that James almost crashed into her.

'I wish you wouldn't do that,' James grumbled.

'Sorry,' Mandy said absent-mindedly. 'But just think, James, if we hadn't stopped here that day and heard the vixen's cries, Lucky and his mum would never have survived.' Mandy shuddered at the thought.

'But they did,' said James sensibly, 'and we might even see them again. Come on, let's get a move on!'

As soon as they turned into the drive that led up to the huge, old-fashioned house where the sisters lived, James put Blackie's lead on. The sweeping lawns at the front of the house were ready for the first cut of the year. Mandy and James leaned their bikes against the stone wall at the bottom of the steps.

'Now stay, Blackie, stay!' James said firmly. Blackie wagged his tail and sat down obediently beside the bicycles. 'See,' James said proudly, 'he *is* learning.' He hooked the lead over the handlebars of his bike and followed Mandy up the great stone steps.

Mandy knocked on the wooden front door. When it creaked open she saw that both the Spry sisters had come to the door. Miss Marjorie fiddled fussily with a row of pearls round her neck and clutched nervously at her cardigan. Miss Joan hovered in the background. They were twins, and as alike as two peas in a pod.

'Mandy, my dear!' exclaimed Miss Marjorie. 'How nice to see you.'

'And James,' finished Miss Joan. The elderly sisters lived alone in The Riddings but since Mandy and James had persuaded them to adopt Patch, one of their school cat's kittens, they had been gradually getting a little bit more involved with village life. Everyone admired the way they had stood up to Sam Western over the foxhunting issue in the village. Mandy had proved to the sisters that Sam Western was responsible for setting traps to kill foxes, and they had refused to support his hunting plans, banishing him from their land.

'Hello, Miss Marjorie, Miss Joan,' Mandy said warmly. 'Oh look, James, Patch has come to see us.' She bent down and ran her hand over the little cat's sleek fur.

'See how big he's grown,' Miss Joan said. 'Isn't he doing well?' Patch stretched out his front paws and yawned.

'What a good home you have here, Patch,' Mandy told him, rubbing him behind his ears and making him purr. The sisters blushed with pleasure as Mandy and James stroked their pet, who was their pride and joy.

'I'm sure you young people didn't come here just to see Patch,' Miss Marjorie said. 'What can we do for you?'

'We're going to be helping to make a programme about foxes,' Mandy said proudly, 'and we need to do some research. Could we look for foxes on your land, please?'

Miss Marjorie's face lit up with a smile. 'How exciting, Mandy,' she said. 'Will it be like *Wildlife Ways*? We always listen to that on our wireless.'

She stepped out of the doorway, her birdlike face pale in the sunshine.

'It *is Wildlife Ways*, but it will be on television,' Mandy told them.

'Television!' Miss Marjorie gasped, as if Mandy had said she was going to the moon.

'Television!' echoed her sister. 'Father didn't approve of new-fangled things like television.' Miss Joan frowned. 'He said it was a five-minute wonder that would never catch on. So we've stuck with the wireless.'

'But foxes, you say, Mandy?' Miss Marjorie had recovered from her shock. She came out further on to the top step and bent closer to Mandy and James. 'We see quite a lot of foxes up here.' She clenched her hands and looked around furtively, as if she expected Sam Western to pop up out of the flowerbed. 'Almost every evening we see them coming and going. *Last* evening there was one on the lawn.'

Mandy's heart leaped. She grinned at James who gave a little whistle. 'That *does* sound promising,' he said, nodding.

Not to be outdone, Miss Joan came out on to the step next to her sister. 'I've seen *lots* of foxes early in the mornings too. More than you!' she announced, pushing in front of her sister.

Suddenly there was a crash of bicycles hitting the ground. Blackie had 'stayed' long enough. He was heading for the steps, dragging James's bike behind him with his lead. As the bike caught on the bottom step, the lead slipped off the handlebars and freed Blackie. He bounded up the steps, eager to say hello to the Spry sisters. Mandy quickly jumped in front of the sisters so that Blackie didn't knock them down like skittles. Patch gave a screech and Miss Joan scooped him up in her arms.

The Labrador was almost at the top of the steps before James stopped him with an impressive flying tackle. They rolled back down, landing in a tangled heap at the bottom.

Nobody moved for a very long moment. The Spry sisters stared at the scene in astonishment. Patch now clung around Miss Joan's neck like an old-fashioned fur collar, with his tail up in the air.

Finally, holding tightly to Blackie's lead, James scrambled to his feet. He picked up his cap and pushed his glasses back up his nose, brushing off some of the dust now covering his clothes.

Blackie looked really pleased with himself. He

danced on the lead and looked eagerly up the steps as if expecting everyone's approval.

'Sorry about that,' James said, scarlet with embarrassment. 'He's um, well, not quite fully trained yet.'

Now that Mandy was over the initial shock of seeing it happen and realised that James and Blackie weren't hurt, it was all she could do not to burst out laughing.

'Um, perhaps we should think about getting back now.' James glanced pleadingly at Mandy. 'We don't want to miss Michelle this evening.'

'We'll come back early tomorrow morning,' Mandy promised the Spry sisters. 'That is, if that's all right with you?'

'Fine, fine. Help yourselves, go wherever you want,' Miss Marjorie replied.

Mandy said a hurried goodbye to Patch, who was just beginning to unwind himself from Miss Joan's neck.

'Good luck,' the Spry sisters called in unison, before hurrying inside and shutting the door firmly behind them.

'Are you OK?' Mandy asked when she got to the bottom of the steps.

'Yep. Fine,' James said shortly.

Mandy began to giggle. 'That dog is getting

worse, not better! You did look funny rolling down the steps.'

'I bet,' James said ruefully, bending down to pull out a bit of twig that was stuck in Blackie's collar. 'What am I going to do with you, Blackie?' he laughed, patting the dog's head.

'He just likes being with you, that's all,' Mandy said, picking up James's bike and wheeling it to him.

They cycled back down to the village and left Blackie at James's house, then made their way over to Animal Ark. They left their bikes and went into reception. It was empty; Jean had obviously gone home. But there was a light under the door of one of the examination rooms.

Mandy pushed the door open. Emily Hope was putting a jar of ointment into a cupboard while Adam Hope was pouring disinfectant into a spray bottle from a plastic drum.

'Hi, Mum, Hi, Dad. We went up to The Riddings. We can begin our search for foxes on the Spry sisters' land first thing tomorrow morning,' Mandy said, flopping into a chair. 'I bet Michelle will be pleased.'

James wedged his cap in his jacket pocket and perched on a stool. 'They've seen lots of foxes,' he told them. 'Even on the lawn. So let's hope it'll be easy for us.'

'Don't be disheartened if you *don't* find foxes instantly, you two,' Adam Hope said, crossing the room with a pile of patients' files in his arms. 'Remember the process of elimination.'

Mandy looked puzzled. 'What d' you mean?'

'Like detective work?' questioned James.

'Exactly,' Mandy's dad said, handing the files to Emily Hope. 'It's just as important to record where there *aren't* any signs of foxes. Then you can gradually build up an understanding of the kind of places foxes favour and you'll be able to make a map of the areas that they *do* use.'

'Oh, I see,' Mandy said slowly as she grasped the idea. 'So if we spent a whole morning and didn't see any signs it wouldn't be a waste of time?'

'That's it,' Mr Hope nodded. 'And speaking of wild animals, I'm going to check on the hedgehog I operated on this afternoon.' He raised his eyebrows at Mandy and James. 'Want to come?'

'You bet!' Mandy said with a firm nod. 'Is it going to be all right?'

'Fine,' her dad answered. 'You both know how

hardy hedgehogs are. Their ability to survive is quite amazing.'

Mandy and James followed Mr Hope through to the residential unit at the back of Animal Ark. This was where domestic animals recovering from operations or in for observation were kept overnight. An annexe had been set up for wild animals. Simon was just finishing up his rounds.

'Hi, you two,' he said, looking up from rolling a bandage. 'How's it going?'

'Great,' Mandy told him. Michelle's coming at half past six to tell us what she wants us to do for the *Wildlife Ways* programme.

'Look at this little fellow,' Adam Hope said, gently picking up the hedgehog. 'He's had a real bashing. The postman found him; he reckoned his head had been cut by a strimmer. His ear was hanging off when he arrived, so we had to remove it completely.' He pointed to the neat row of stitches where an ear should have been, and a big sore area behind with a scab on it.

'Will he be able to be released back into the wild?' Mandy asked, her voice full of concern.

'He should be right as rain,' her dad said. 'We'll just keep him in until the stitches come out and the scab comes off.' He put the hedgehog back. 'Now, I'm going to go and put my feet up, I'm whacked.' He put an arm round each of Mandy and James's shoulders and pretended to collapse on them.

'Da-ad! You're too heavy!' Mandy cried. She and James staggered along in fits of giggles, dragging him through to the kitchen, where they fell into chairs around the big, wooden kitchen table.

Mandy could hardly wait for Michelle to arrive, so she could tell them all about the programme. She wanted to start work on it right away.

Two

'Hi, everyone,' Michelle called. She had arrived just as Emily Hope was pouring out steaming mugs of hot chocolate.

'Hi, Michelle,' said Mandy. 'Come and have some chocolate.'

Michelle gratefully took the mug Mandy offered her and put her shoulder bag on the floor. She was a slim woman, not a lot taller than Mandy, with short, glossy brown hair. She was wearing khaki trousers that had lots of useful zipped pockets and a cream cotton shirt with the sleeves rolled up. Her dangly silver earrings tinkled when she turned her head.

'We've been so busy, I haven't stopped all

day,' Michelle told them as she took off her coat. She took a folder full of papers out of her bag and sat down at the table. 'So, how are my two helpers getting on? Any ideas on where we should start looking?' she asked Mandy and James. 'I am *so* excited about this project. I reckon we're going to make a really good film.'

'We went up to the Spry sisters' house this afternoon to ask permission to look on their land. We thought we could start searching for foxes tomorrow morning,' Mandy said. 'Miss Marjorie says the foxes sometimes come right up into their garden.'

'Foxes have large territories,' Michelle informed them. 'What I'd like you to look for is a breeding earth,' she carried on.

'How will we recognise it?' Mandy asked.

'Foxes usually have several earths on their territory but the vixen picks only one to breed in,' Michelle said, stopping to take a sip of her chocolate. 'Mmm, that's good! The cubs will stay in or around the breeding earth. The vixen will only move them before that if she's disturbed.'

'Do they drag leaves and stuff inside for a nest, like hedgehogs?' Mandy asked.

'Or collect fresh hay, like badgers?' James asked.

'It's interesting you should ask that. Foxes don't actually make a nest at all,' Michelle told them, warming to her subject. 'The vixen gives birth to the cubs straight on to the bare earth. For the first two weeks of life the cubs are too small to keep themselves warm so the vixen can't leave them at all.'

'How does she manage to eat?' James asked, picking up a biscuit from the plate in the middle of the table.

'Trust you to think of food, James!' Mandy said. James was *always* hungry.

'It's sensible question,' Emily Hope said, defending James as they all laughed. She sat down with them at the table. 'Foxes live in family groups, usually mum, dad and the cubs. But there are often other adult foxes in the group too, older brothers and sisters, and they will help to bring her food. Mostly it's the dog fox that brings most of the food.'

'So foxes aren't that different from us!' Mandy said, grinning at her mum.

Michelle nodded. 'Now, I'm not going to be able to start looking at sites until Monday evening. We've got to have the film ready to edit by the weekend, so if you two would like to make a start tomorrow, I'll give you some tips for fox-watching,' she said.

Mandy and James leaned forward.

'First of all, you have to stay as invisible as possible. A country fox is one of the hardest animals to get close to. Once you find an earth that's in use, position yourselves downwind of it. A fox's sense of smell is strong. Don't use insect repellent or take strong smelling food or drink with you. And don't forget that a fox's hearing is excellent – they can hear a mouse moving when it's nearly three metres away. So, you'll need to be even quieter than mice. For example, don't wear clothes that rustle. And you know not to wear brightly coloured clothes.'

Mandy nodded enthusiastically. 'So tomorrow morning should we start by looking for an earth?' she asked.

'Yes, please. If you can find a breeding earth, that would be great,' Michelle said. 'Foxes are amazingly clever, they will adapt anything suitable to use as an earth.'

'How will Mandy and James know if the earth is in use?' Emily Hope asked.

'There are a couple of giveaways,' Michelle told them. 'The cubs will be old enough to be playing outside now, so the grass will be flattened. You'll see lots of animal bones, feathers, remains of meals and other bits and pieces. I think you would certainly notice the mess! But you'll see most activity early in the morning and in the evenings.'

'You two will be out from dawn to dusk then,' Mrs Hope said to Mandy and James. She picked up the plate of biscuits and offered them to Michelle.

'I think we should start as early as possible,' Mandy decided. 'About five o'clock?'

James looked aghast at the thought of getting up so early on the first day of the holidays.

'The earlier the better, James,' Michelle advised, collecting her papers together and standing up. 'Let's hope it's not pouring with rain!'

'I think the forecast for tomorrow is fine,' Simon said, as he joined them in the kitchen.

'So that's all settled, then. See you Monday evening at five-thirty,' Michelle said, getting up to leave.

'Just a moment, Michelle,' Emily Hope said, as she collected all the mugs. 'I hate to be a spoilsport, Mandy, but what about your work at Animal Ark? Simon can't *keep* doing all your jobs for you,' she reminded her.

'I'll help,' offered James. Mandy shot him a grateful look.

'If James helps me, we could do any jobs in the residential unit before the dusk watch,' she said, looking pleadingly at her mother.

'I'm happy to do any extra jobs while this project is on, Mandy,' Simon said generously, 'but . . .' There was a wicked glint in his eye. 'When it's over . . .'

'I'll do anything you like,' Mandy begged with a grin. 'All the jobs you don't like doing, for as long as you want.'

'You're on!' Simon agreed. 'And I'll keep you to it.'

Mandy showed Michelle to the door. 'Bye, everyone,' she called over her shoulder as she went out. 'I'll see you on Monday!'

As soon as Mandy's alarm went off, she sprang out of bed. Within minutes she was dressed, downstairs and drinking a glass of milk from the fridge. Mandy closed the front door quietly behind her, so as not to wake her parents, and soon she was pedalling down the lane on her bike to meet James outside the post office, as they'd arranged.

They cycled towards The Riddings in silence, both deep in thought. Taking a short cut to the sisters' land, they left their bikes in the bushes and set off on foot.

At the bottom of the meadow an old path led through a wood of old, gnarled beech trees. A sprinkling of rain the previous night had made the earth damp. As they trod through the undergrowth of springy ferns, squirrels scrambled up tree trunks to peer down at them from a safe height.

Deep among the trees, Mandy and James came to a rickety plank bridge that crossed a narrow stream, marking the edge of the Spry sisters' land. They crossed it and headed up towards the open moors.

Suddenly James stopped and sniffed. 'Foxes!' he said softly. 'I think they've been here recently, marking their territory.'

Mandy could smell a strong scent in the air, something like a mixture of wood varnish, cheese and smelly socks. You could hardly miss it.

'Walter taught me to recognise that foxy smell,' James whispered to Mandy, as he studied the muddy track for telltale signs. Quickly he found what he was looking for. 'Mandy, look, here in the mud!'

Mandy peered to where he was pointing. She saw a clearly-defined set of prints crossing the path, narrower in shape than those made by a dog.

'These are fresh,' observed James, 'made since it rained, probably in the night or even this morning. And look, here are some more.'

Further on they found tufts of long fur caught on a bramble bush. With a surge of excitement, Mandy picked off some to take back and show her parents. She was sure the reddish fur belonged to a fox. She gazed at the great prickly mass of brambles that extended for several metres in all directions. 'This is exactly the sort of place Michelle said foxes would use,' Mandy breathed, getting down on all fours to peer underneath. There was no way that either she or James could crawl under the brambles to have a look. 'But there's nothing around to show it's an earth, is there?' Mandy noted. 'Have a look round the other side, James.'

James waded through the bracken surrounding the prickly bush. 'I can't see anything,' he said, after he'd walked right round. 'No feathers or bones. But I can't see right into the middle.' James looked thoughtful. 'You know, foxes can squeeze through a hole less than ten centimetres across.' He made a shape with his hands. 'Imagine a big dog fox getting through a gap not much bigger than a cricket ball.'

'There could easily be foxes in there, then,' Mandy said. 'It's a good safe place for them, isn't it?' She was feeling optimistic. 'Let's watch for a while. If we're really still and quiet they might come back.'

A short distance away, they found a fallen tree and sat down to watch the bramble patch. In silence they waited for nearly half an hour, but not a single fox passed by.

'Let's move on,' Mandy suggested, her enthusiasm ebbing. After they had discovered the footprints and the fur, she had felt sure there were foxes nearby.

Mandy and James worked their way through the woods, noting down any signs of foxes they saw along the way.

They walked out on to the moor and scanned the foreground. Suddenly, James tugged at her sleeve. Mandy looked to where he was pointing across the moor. A fox was crossing the rise above them!

Mandy hardly dared to breathe as she slowly raised her binoculars. She watched as it ran

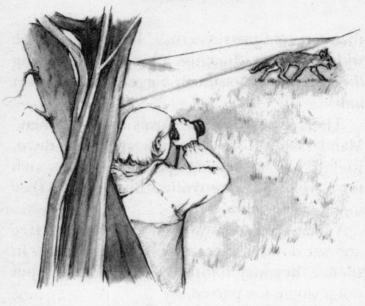

along the crest, then stopped, head up, ears twitching, sniffing the air. Then it was off again across the moor where it disappeared into Piper's Wood.

'Do you realise where that fox must have come from?' James said softly, staring at Mandy as he waited for realisation to dawn on her.

Mandy thought. Next to The Riddings' land was . . . 'Oh no, James! It came from the direction of Upper Welford Hall,' she said in a faint voice.

James nodded. 'Sam Western's place,' he groaned. 'We know how much *he* cares about wildlife. He and Dennis Saville will shoot anything that moves.'

Mandy nodded grimly. She and James had already had several run-ins with Sam Western and his gamekeeper Dennis Saville. The two men had poisoned one of Lydia Fawcett's goats and had been responsible for setting the traps that had nearly killed Lucky and his mother.

'If Sam Western found foxes on his land,' James voiced her thoughts, 'he'd be sure to want to start a foxhunt again.'

Mandy felt her heart jolt. 'And James! Remember what he did last year?' she said, gripping her handlebars so hard that her knuckles turned white.

'Yes,' James said, his mouth setting into a grim line. 'He organised the local farmers into a hunting party to get rid of the foxes.' He stared angrily in the direction of Upper Welford Hall.

'And they shot an innocent dog fox,' Mandy said grimly. She remembered how they had found the poor dead fox that Sam Western had shot for fear it would steal his pheasants. What if he found out that there were foxes on his land again? 'We'll have to make sure he doesn't find out about Michelle filming around here,' she told James. 'We can't put the foxes in danger.'

*   *   *

The sun was growing warm as Mandy and James cycled back and a cool breeze began to blow away unpleasant thoughts about Sam Western. Morning surgery was finished when Mandy and James arrived at Animal Ark. They got stuck into Mandy's daily tasks straight away. James swept the floor, while Mandy fetched fresh bedding for the patients in the residential unit.

'We saw a fox near Piper's Wood,' Mandy told her parents, as she and James worked. She remembered the fur she had brought home. 'And we found this,' she said, taking it out of her pocket and showing it to her dad.

'Yes, that's fox fur,' he confirmed. 'These long hairs are called the guard hairs. Foxes begin their moult about this time of year and they can look very ragged. Fascinating creatures, foxes. You two are going to enjoy this, aren't you?'

Mandy nodded happily. 'We plan to take Blackie for a walk this afternoon and then go straight back to Piper's Wood to look for an earth,' she told him as she finished tidying up.

After lunch, Mandy and James took Blackie

down to the river and let him off the lead. They sat on the warm sand, whilst Blackie raced along the riverbank.

'I've made a note of everything we've seen so far connected with foxes,' Mandy said, chewing the end of her pencil and squinting. 'When we go tonight,' she declared confidently, 'we can fill in exactly where we find the earth. Then Michelle can start filming right away on Monday.' She sprang to her feet, brushed the sand from her trousers and handed her notebook to James.

'*If* we find it!' James reminded her, looking through her notes. 'It's not a hundred per cent certain that we will.'

'We will, James,' Mandy smiled. 'I know we will.'

At that moment Blackie, who had decided to take a dip, came bounding out of the river towards them. 'Aaargh, look out, James!' Mandy warned, jumping out of range, but it was too late. Blackie shook himself vigorously, spraying James from head to toe with droplets of water.

'Oh, thanks, Blackie,' James laughed. 'I was feeling a bit warm.'

'Come on,' Mandy said, laughing. 'Let's take Blackie home and then we can start.'

*   *   *

The late afternoon sun was on their backs as
they cycled up the lane to Piper's Wood. In the
distance they could just make out the ivy-clad
walls of Upper Welford Hall, Sam Western's
house. Mandy stuck her arm out to signal to
James and veered off down a track. She stopped
beside a stile. 'Let's leave our bikes here,' she
said.

They left their bikes against a wooden post.
Then they searched through the rest of the
woods, carefully checking out any possible
places that a fox might use as an earth. They
were so busy with their project that they
hardly realised it had begun to get dark.
Eventually, Mandy flopped down on an old
tree trunk. 'OK,' she sighed. 'What have we
got so far?'

'Not much, really,' James shrugged. 'Two
disused earths and one possibly in use.'

'Just because you found an empty take-away
box,' Mandy teased, 'doesn't mean it's possibly
in use.'

'No, I know,' James blushed.

'We'll just have to keep searching,' Mandy said
in a resigned voice. 'Nobody said it would be
easy.'

'I didn't think it would be this hard though,' James acknowledged. 'They certainly know how to hide themselves.'

'We'd better start back soon,' Mandy said, looking around. 'It's beginning to get dark.'

James led the way as they hurried back to their bikes. 'There's the stile,' he said, climbing over to collect their bikes.

'Oh no, I forgot to get a new battery for my front light,' groaned Mandy, looking along the dark lane.

'I'll go in front, then you can take mine when we reach my house,' James offered.

All of a sudden, out of the darkness of the wood came a bloodcurdling scream. Then another, closer now.

'What's that?' Mandy cried. 'It sounds like someone's being murdered!' She was not easily spooked but it sent a cold shiver through her.

James face split in a grin from ear to ear. 'That's foxes!' he exclaimed. 'Mandy, they *are* here.'

Three

'Why did the foxes have to wait until it was time for us to go home?' Mandy said. She sat on her bike and looked longingly back at the wood. The eerie screams came again. 'Right James,' Mandy's eyes flashed. 'Tomorrow we're going to find them!'

When they reached James's house they arranged to meet the next morning. 'I'll come here for you, if you like,' Mandy called, as she sped off. 'That will give you five minutes more in bed!' Laughing, she set off for Animal Ark.

Mandy was just passing under the oak tree by the village pond when she spied Walter Pickard crossing the village green. She swerved and rode over to him.

'Hi, Mr Pickard,' Mandy called, as she drew near.

'Hello, young Mandy, what's bringing you this way?' Walter Pickard stopped and waited till Mandy reached him. 'Are you looking for your Grandad? It's bell-ringing practice tonight.'

'No, I'm just on my way home. James and I have been looking for foxes,' she explained, stopping to take a breath. 'Maybe you could help us? We've just been up at Piper's Wood.'

'Aye, but did you see 'em there?' Walter rocked on the heels of his shoes.

'Not yet,' Mandy said, shaking her head. 'We found old earths and heard some foxes scream but . . .' Then the words all spilled out and soon she had told him the whole story about the film and the urgent need to find a breeding earth. 'And we're looking again tomorrow morning,' Mandy finished. 'We haven't much time and we don't want to let Michelle down.'

Walter Pickard gazed down at Mandy with a long, thoughtful look. 'There's been foxes breeding in Piper's Wood since I was a lad,' he told her. 'But not many people knows where to look. That's what keeps 'em safe.'

'I bet *you* know where to look, Mr Pickard?' Mandy said, knowing full well he did, but trying to flatter him into helping them.

'Aye, happen I do,' Walter said, nodding slowly. He hesitated for a few more seconds then made his decision. 'You tell young James to look where I showed him the mushrooms that time,' Walter told her. 'But make sure nobody else knows.'

Mandy beamed. 'Thank you, Mr Pickard, you won't regret it.'

'Eh-up, here comes Ernie Bell, he'll expect me to have the church opened up by now,' Walter said, drawing himself up. 'Mind what I said, now, about keeping the information to yourselves.'

'I will,' Mandy nodded. 'And thanks.' She waved to Ernie Bell and set off down the lane towards home. Pedalling fast and furiously, Mandy almost collided with a camper van as it came slowly around the bend.

'Hello, Mandy love,' her grandad said, winding down the window. 'You're in a hurry. Are you late for something?'

Mandy laughed. 'No, but you are, Grandad! Walter Pickard and Ernie Bell are already at the church.'

'I thought they might be. I was watching the sunset with your gran. It's a real shepherd's sunset.' He gazed back the way he'd come. The sky was flame red with streaks of gold where the sun was slipping below the horizon.

'Red sky at night, shepherd's delight,' Mandy recited. 'That's good. James and I are off at dawn to search for foxes. Walter Pickard has told us where to look!' Mandy told him.

'Well if anybody knows, it'll be Walter.' A peal of bells rang out. 'Oops! I'd better get a move on,' Grandad said guiltily.

'Bye, Grandad,' Mandy called as he pulled away.

Mandy skidded to a halt on the drive outside Animal Ark, put her bike away and rushed up the steps to reception, eager to tell her parents the good news.

'Dad and I had an idea, too,' Emily Hope said, after Mandy had told them all about her afternoon. 'As you don't have much time, why don't you ask Mrs Ponsonby if the people involved with Fox Watch have seen any vixens with cubs?' She wiped the table down. 'I know that when she started Fox Watch Mrs Ponsonby had the wrong intentions. Driving the foxes out wasn't quite the right idea!' She gave Mandy a wry smile. 'But she did come good in the end.'

'Fox Watch!' Mandy's face lit up. 'That's a brilliant idea, Mum. Why didn't I think of that?'

'You just have incredibly brilliant parents,' Adam Hope joked. 'Don't forget it was me who convinced Mrs Ponsonby that saving foxes was saving part of our natural heritage.'

'Oh!' Mandy's face fell.

'What's wrong?' Mrs Hope asked, rinsing her hands.

'Well, Fox Watch is a great idea . . .' Mandy faltered.

'I sense a "but" coming now.' Adam Hope had a twinkle in his eye.

'It's just that Mrs Ponsonby, she's so . . . so . . .' Mandy floundered around for a polite word. 'Forceful! She takes over everything.'

'Now, Mandy, don't be unkind,' Emily Hope said. 'She may be forceful, as you say, but she certainly gets things done. And she's not afraid to stand up to people.'

Mandy looked to her dad for support but he was feeling generous too. 'She's not so bad, Mandy,' he agreed. 'She's all huff and puff but underneath it all, she means well.'

'Go on, Mandy,' Emily Hope said, putting all

the surgical instruments into the steriliser and turning it on. 'Go and call her now.'

Mandy waited while the phone rang at Bleakfell Hall, the huge Victorian mansion where Mrs Ponsonby lived.

'Hello, Bleakfell Hall, the Ponsonby residence,' a voice said. Mandy stifled a laugh. She could hear Pandora, Mrs Ponsonby's Pekinese, yapping noisily, and Toby, her mongrel, barking excitedly.

'Hello, Mrs Ponsonby, it's Mandy Hope here,' she said.

'Oh, Mandy dear!' exclaimed Mrs Ponsonby. 'Hold on a moment.'

Mandy waited as the yapping got louder and louder. Eventually it sounded as though the dogs were yapping straight down the phone.

'Pandora wants to say hello,' Mrs Ponsonby told her. Mandy moved the phone away from her head as Pandora yapped in her ear. 'Do say hello to her, then she'll be quiet.'

'Hello, Pandora,' Mandy said, pulling a face as she saw her mum and dad standing at the surgery door, grinning.

'Good. Now, what can I do for you, Mandy?' Mrs Ponsonby said, as if chatting to a dog on the phone was perfectly normal. However, Mrs

Ponsonby had been right – Pandora had stopped yapping.

'Well, it's about Fox Watch.' Mandy proceeded to tell Mrs Ponsonby all about the programme and finding foxes. 'Dad wondered if you had seen any cubs recently?'

'I'm sure we should be able to help, Mandy,' Mrs Ponsonby said happily. 'We haven't been meeting much lately, I have to say. Everybody was so busy with the Easter celebrations,' she continued. 'But I will get in touch with the rest of the group and see if there's any news. How would that be?'

'Fine,' Mandy answered, feeling a bit disappointed that Mrs Ponsonby didn't have anything to tell her now. 'Thank you very much,' she added, remembering her manners.

'Mandy! Before you go,' Mrs Ponsonby called down the telephone. 'I expect they will want to interview *me* for the film – in my capacity as head of Fox Watch, of course. Perhaps I should come along to the filming? Meet the producer and give them some tips? I do know quite a lot about foxes now, dear.'

Mandy was horrified. 'I'll tell Michelle,' she said in a strangled voice. 'It's up to her. Bye.'

Mandy replaced the receiver and turned to

her parents. 'She wants to be in the film!' she spluttered. Adam and Emily Hope were leaning against the door, laughing at Mandy's shocked expression.

'Don't worry, Michelle will sort Mrs Ponsonby out,' Adam Hope reassured her.

'I hope so,' Mandy gulped. 'Now I'd better ring James and tell him the good news.'

But when James came to the phone he was puzzled. 'Mushrooms? I don't remember any mushrooms. Didn't he say anything else?' he quizzed Mandy.

'No. James you'll have to think hard,' Mandy said in a pleading voice. 'This is our big chance. You *have* to remember!' They said goodbye and Mandy hung up. Her face was set into a frown.

'Give him time, love,' her dad said cheerfully. 'He'll probably remember by the morning.'

It was still dark when the alarm rang next morning. Mandy reached out and switched it off. She was still so tired by all the excitement of the day before that she promptly fell asleep again.

'Mandy, wake up, love.' Emily Hope shook her gently and switched on the bedside light.

Mandy sat up with a start. 'Oh Mum,' she said, rubbing her eyes. 'I've been gathering mushrooms in my sleep all night!'

Emily Hope gave her a broad, warm smile. 'Did you dream where the foxes were too?' Her green eyes crinkled with amusement.

Mandy grinned. 'I wish it was that easy,' she declared, jumping out of bed and throwing on her clothes. 'I told James I'd be extra early today.'

'Now take it easy, it's not five yet,' her mum replied. 'I'm going to grab another hour's sleep. Mind how you go.'

'Okay, thanks Mum.' Mandy flew downstairs, grabbed an apple from the fruit bowl on the way out and put on her cycling helmet.

Dawn was breaking as Mandy saw James coming towards her down the drive. They had arranged to meet at the front gate, so as not to disturb the rest of the Hunter household.

'Have you remembered anything?' she asked excitedly.

'Nope.' James shook his head dolefully. 'Zilch.'

'Perhaps it will come to you when we get there,' Mandy said positively, as they set off on their bikes towards Piper's Wood.

When they reached the stile, they left their bikes and stood at the edge of the wood. 'Which way?' Mandy asked.

'I don't know.' James looked gloomy. 'I mean, when they're out, the whole wood is full of mushrooms, they grow everywhere.'

Mandy looked around anxiously. James was right. 'Well, could it be a special mushroom, something unusual?' she asked.

James looked down at his shoes and scratched his head. 'That's it!' he suddenly exclaimed. 'Follow me.' He began to stride away into the wood.

Mandy could hardly keep up as James trekked through the wood up towards the moor. Suddenly he put up his arm in a halt position. 'It will be around here somewhere,' he said confidently.

'How do you know?' Mandy asked, puzzled.

'Trust me!' James answered. 'And start looking.'

Where the moor met the wood there was an area of scrubland that was covered with bramble and long, tufty grass. They began their search for evidence of foxes.

Eventually, James spotted what he was looking for and sighed happily. He looked across at

Mandy, who nodded. She'd spotted it too. Halfway up the sloping bank was a small burrow. The grass all around it was trodden down. There were bits of bone scattered around, and scraps of plastic bags and paper here and there. Now they just needed proof it was occupied.

'Please let's see a fox,' Mandy breathed, crossing her fingers.

Downwind of the earth they waited. And waited, and waited.

Mandy was just beginning to lose hope, when she noticed something moving a little way off. Coming down from a rise with a rabbit in its mouth she saw a fox, its golden red fur shimmering as it ran. Its tail was the same length as its body, and was tipped with white. They watched it reach the earth and look around suspiciously. Its amber eyes seemed to stare right at them before it disappeared down the burrow.

'It's not very big, but it looks mature,' James whispered in Mandy's ear. 'I think it's a vixen.'

'Good,' she whispered back. 'Then it's more than likely there'll be cubs.'

As they watched, the vixen came out again and settled herself on the grass beside a bramble bush near to the earth. Mandy held her breath as a movement at the mouth of the burrow caught her eye. Still wobbly on its legs, a tiny cub came out of the earth. It stumbled and then tripped over a bramble, falling on its snout and rolling over on to its back, mewing sorrowfully.

'Is it hurt?' Mandy mouthed to James. James shook his head.

Legs waving in the air, the cub threw itself on to its side and staggered to its feet. Just then another cub came out and chased after the first one. The two cubs ran towards each other and collided, tumbled over each other and landed

in a heap. Both cubs still had their chocolate-coloured first coat, but patches of bright reddish-orange fur just showed through where they'd begun to moult. One cub had an edge of white fur around the tip of its ear; the other had grey flecks on its right forefoot. The cubs sat up, blinked in the light and mewed for their mother. The vixen got up and immediately herded the cubs back down the burrow. In silence, Mandy and James crept away. It was only when they were out of earshot that they spoke.

Mandy was elated. 'We've done it, James, we've found a breeding earth! Weren't the cubs gorgeous?'

'Really sweet,' James agreed, smiling. 'It was funny when they bumped into each other.'

'How old do you think they are?' Mandy asked, as they reached the stile.

'A few weeks?' James suggested thoughtfully. 'Their eyes were amber, not blue any more. Remember how Lucky's eyes changed colour?'

Mandy vaulted the stile and stood grinning at him. 'You're brilliant! Now, what I want to know is what made you suddenly remember where to look?'

'Actually,' James said, turning pink with pleasure, 'it was when you said about a special mushroom. That's when I remembered. I was out with the Welford Wildlifers bird-watching. Walter called me over and showed me a place where all these mushrooms that looked like white tennis balls were growing. They're called puffballs. I remembered that they were by the edge of the wood and there was a big dead tree nearby.'

'Michelle is going to be so pleased,' Mandy said, her face full of excitement.

James grinned. 'I wonder if Michelle will start filming tonight?' he said.

'I hope so,' Mandy replied, sitting astride her bike. 'I can't wait!'

Four

'So Michelle's going to start the actual filming tonight, then?' Emily Hope said, as she whizzed round the kitchen preparing lunch for the family.

'I hope so,' Mandy nodded. 'We've found a breeding earth so we don't need to spend any more time looking. She and Janie, she's the camera operator, said they will collect James and me at about half-past five.' She was sitting at the big kitchen table cleaning her binoculars with a soft cloth. 'That will give them plenty of time to set up the camera and get everything ready before the vixen starts hunting for the night.' Mandy put her binoculars down on the kitchen table. 'You should have seen the cubs, Mum, they're *gorgeous*.'

Adam Hope came through the door that connected the surgery to the cottage. 'Simon said he might pop up and have a look sometime,' he said. 'That is if you'll still be up there when he finishes work?'

'Oh, I should think we will,' Mandy said, nodding her head vigorously. 'Michelle is hoping to film all night. By the way, is it all right if I stay out with her?'

Mandy's mum and dad exchanged looks and then Mr Hope nodded. 'But you'll be falling asleep on your feet,' her dad teased.

'Not me, Dad,' Mandy retorted, jumping up to lay the table. 'Not with foxes to watch, no way!'

Emily Hope put a big bowl of homemade vegetable soup on the table. 'There's bread in the oven, Mandy, could you fetch it for me please?' she said, gently stirring the soup with a ladle. 'Mind you don't burn yourself, it's hot!'

Mandy got a clean cloth and carefully took a crusty loaf of granary bread out of the hot oven. 'I'm starving!' she announced.

'I'm not surprised,' Mrs Hope laughed. 'I bet you didn't eat any breakfast.'

'I had an apple,' Mandy replied, putting the loaf on the breadboard and taking the butter from the fridge. 'James is coming over after lunch and we'll do all my chores before Michelle arrives.'

'The energy of the girl!' Adam Hope said, feigning exhaustion. 'Where does she get it all?'

Mandy grinned and tucked into her soup. Finding the foxes had filled her with excitement and she couldn't wait to start on the filming. She ate her lunch and took her bowl over to the sink. 'Right, I've got time to do my jobs in the residential unit before Simon gets back from lunch,' she announced. 'Any new patients?'

'One pet rabbit in with a broken leg. The ginger cat with the poisoned foot has been discharged,' Adam Hope told her. 'Lucky for you we're not run off our feet at the moment.'

'And for Simon!' Emily Hope added.

In the residential unit Mandy put on an apron. Her job was to check that every animal had a clean bed or litter tray and a bowl of fresh water to drink. She worked her way around the room, checking on the rabbit with the bandaged leg. It lay still and half asleep, its leg straight out in front of it. 'You're quite comfortable, I can see,' Mandy told it, gently stroking its ears.

James was late but Mandy didn't mind. She loved her work at Animal Ark and being busy made the time pass quickly.

'Sorry, Mandy,' James said sheepishly when he eventually arrived. 'I fell asleep and Mum thought I needed a rest, so she didn't wake me up!'

'That's OK. You're here now. I've nearly finished,' Mandy said. She was just taking off her apron when there was a 'toot' from the drive.

'That's them!' James said eagerly.

Grabbing their coats, they raced through reception and down the steps to Michelle's Jeep. Emily Hope came out of the cottage carrying Mandy's binoculars, a big Thermos flask of hot chocolate and hefty slices of Gran's fruitcake for them all.

'That should keep you going for a while,' she said. 'Good luck.'

'Thanks, Mum.' Mandy planted a kiss on her mum's cheek and jumped in the back beside James.

Michelle rolled down her window. 'I'll get them back safe and sound in the morning, after what I hope will be a good night's filming,' she said cheerfully. 'If you need to contact us, Simon knows where we'll be. And tell him I'll shoot him if he makes a noise and disturbs our foxes!' She laughed and started the engine.

The woman in the passenger seat turned to face Mandy and James and introduced herself. 'Hi, I'm Janie, the camera operator for this project.' Janie had cropped bleached hair and friendly brown eyes.

'Janie's a brilliant camera operator,' Michelle put in.

'What sort of camera do you use?' asked James, who was always interested in the technical details.

'It's an E.N.G. type camera with a sun-gun and image intensification,' Janie told him.

'That sounds complicated,' James said. 'What does E.N.G. stand for?'

'Electronic News Gathering, and it's not at all complicated. It's the same sort they use to make the outside broadcast TV news,' Janie went on eagerly. 'Hand-held, and with no extra wires or lights. It makes me a one-man band. It's brilliant.'

Michelle slowed down and pulled the Jeep off the road beside Piper's Wood.

'How far is it from here, Mandy?' she asked, looking at her watch.

'About five minutes,' Mandy said, leaning forward and peering through the windscreen. 'You see where the moor begins to rise from the forest, by that dead tree sticking up higher than the rest?'

'Uh huh.' Michelle nodded.

'It's just there,' James finished.

Mandy and James helped carry the big metal box that contained the camera equipment up to the wood.

When the fox's earth eventually came in sight, Michelle was delighted. 'This is perfect, you two,' she enthused. 'Well done! We can see all we need from here. And once they get used to us and realise we're not dangerous, the foxes won't take too much notice.' Michelle watched the earth through her binoculars for a few moments.

Janie soon set up her equipment and they settled down to wait.

It wasn't long before the vixen emerged from the entrance to the earth. She went to the same patch of grass that Mandy and James had seen her choose earlier that day and lay up in the last of the sunshine. Moments later, the first cub toddled out of the entrance, closely followed by the second.

Mandy had to resist the urge to gasp as a third, and then a fourth cub followed. It was even better than they had originally thought. Four cubs! She watched in delight as the cubs scampered around their mother and rolled about in the grass.

After a while, the light began to fade and Janie switched on the sun-gun. A filtered light washed over the earth like a ray of sunshine. The vixen immediately stood up and herded her cubs to the entrance of the earth.

Through their binoculars they could see her looking straight at them, fully aware of their presence. Behind her in the darkness of the entrance, four pairs of amber eyes stared unblinkingly at them and four pairs of ears stood straight up and alert. Except for the occasional twitch of a whisker and the trembling of a shiny nose, the four fox cubs stood motionless, watching and waiting for a cue from their mother.

Suddenly she gave a cough and, as if by magic, the cubs vanished down the earth.

Everyone stayed as still as possible. Mandy's heart was thumping. The low whirr of the camera sounded like an aeroplane engine. Surely the vixen must hear it. For several seconds, though it seemed like hours, the vixen watched them. Then she turned and went into the earth. Mandy tried hard to suppress a sigh of relief.

'I think she's accepted us,' Michelle whispered.

'How old are the cubs, Michelle?' Mandy asked quietly.

'I would say these cubs are about five weeks old,' Michelle replied. 'They're beginning to look foxy but their noses haven't turned black yet.'

They continued to watch the earth in silence and after a while the vixen and her cubs emerged above ground again. Mandy couldn't believe her eyes. She looked from Michelle to James. Both looked equally surprised. Now there were not four cubs, but six!

Racing around, they slammed into each other and rolled in the grass. Chasing through the brambles, they danced around the vixen, pulling at her mouth to see if she had any food, until she pushed them away with her snout.

'That means they're hungry,' Michelle said quietly. 'She'll go hunting soon.'

'Look,' breathed James. 'Near the earth, another fox!'

Sure enough, another fox was joining in the

play. It had specks of very dark brown fur round its eyes. Tails wagging and ears drawn flat, the cubs were clambering all over their mother and the new fox, squealing and making clicking noises. All her life Mandy had loved animals, almost more than anything else. But she had never seen such a beautiful sight as this fox family. Both the adult foxes had bright eyes and looked strong and healthy. The cubs were brimming with life, and even though they kept knocking each other over in their boisterous play, they were obviously enjoying it. Mandy and James looked at Michelle. 'Could that be the dog fox?' Mandy asked.

'No. Too small.' Michelle shook her head slowly. 'More likely it's the vixen's daughter from an earlier litter. Last year or even the year before.'

'So she's their big sister?' James suggested.

'Exactly. She's called a "helper",' Michelle told them. 'Foxes are very social creatures. The more foxes there are in a family group to hunt for food, the better the cubs' chances of survival.'

Now the two vixens were herding the cubs to the earth and shooing them inside. Janie switched off the camera and began to change the film.

'How do you think it's looking, Janie?' Mandy asked.

'Fantastic!' Janie grinned. 'We should get some great footage over the next few days.' She had just reset the camera when both vixens appeared at the entrance to the earth. Janie filmed them as they set off to hunt.

The two vixens spent most of the night hunting, bringing back food for the hungry cubs. Michelle had asked Mandy and James to make notes on how many times each vixen hunted and what sort of things they brought back.

By midnight Mandy was beginning to feel really cold from standing still. She zipped up her fleece and carefully moved her aching limbs, edging over to where James was leaning against a tree. 'James!' She nudged him gently.

'Huh!' James started awake and dropped his notebook. 'Phew, Mandy, I was almost asleep,' he confessed.

'I know,' Mandy agreed. 'I'm struggling to keep my eyes open. It's hard to stay awake when it's so quiet.' Mandy was tracking the mother while James noted the helper's movements.

'It's easier when the vixens come back, there's something to do then,' James said. 'Especially for you.'

Just before dawn, Michelle suggested they grab a quick break. 'Have you noticed,' she asked, as they drank the welcome hot chocolate and ate the delicious cake, 'how much more experienced the mother is at hunting?'

'I make it about twelve expeditions for the mother,' Mandy reckoned.

'And about six for the smaller vixen,' James said.

'And the smaller one doesn't bring back so much food, does she?' Mandy added, biting into a chunk of cake.

'She's been bringing back worms and beetles.' James said, 'but the mother seems to be bringing back larger things, like rats.'

'That's right. The younger vixen is still learning from her mum,' Michelle told them as she poured the last of the hot chocolate.

Suddenly, they were all startled by a loud noise. *BOOOM!* The noise rang out from far away on the moors.

'Oh blast!' Michelle smacked her fist into her hand. 'That's someone shooting on the moor!' She sounded really annoyed. 'That will upset our foxes.'

'Not guilty!' they heard a soft voice say behind them.

'It's Simon,' Mandy said, spinning round. 'Where've you been? We thought you'd come up last night.'

'I was too tired, with all that extra work.' He grinned at Mandy's worried expression. 'Only joking. I though I'd get up early this morning before work. How's it going?'

'It was going fine until just now. Did you hear that shot?' Michelle said crossly.

They waited anxiously for any more shots but none came. The young vixen came back with a mouse in her mouth.

'Good!' Michelle breathed softly. 'They obviously weren't bothered by the noise. It was probably just a farmer shooting on his own land.'

'Some poor animal, just getting on with life, but the *farmer* doesn't happen to want it there,' Mandy said angrily.

'So long as the hunters stay on their own land, Mandy,' Simon said, 'like it or not, there's nothing we can do.'

While the cubs squabbled over the mouse, the young vixen went off again.

'They have to work really hard to get enough food for the cubs, don't they?' James said. 'Look! There's the mother!' He pointed at the moor. High on a rise in the last of the moonlight the vixen stood silhouetted against an indigo sky.

Mandy stared at the sight until the vixen turned, and then she had to stifle her laughter. The vixen's head was almost obscured by a large fluffy object. She looked as if she could hardly see over the top of it. 'What on earth has she got this time?' Mandy giggled to James. 'It's enormous.'

James was also trying not to laugh. 'It looks like a pigeon or something.'

'Be quiet, you two!' Michelle pretended to be serious, but she and Janie were smothering their laughter too. 'Let's try and control ourselves, we don't want to frighten her away. It's bigger than a pigeon, anyway,' she added, setting Mandy and James off again.

The vixen began to trot down the moor towards them. She reached the edge of the wood and was melting in and out of the shadows when *BOOOM!* – the gunshot rang out again. But this time the noise was much louder and closer than before.

Mandy felt the blood pounding in her head as she frantically tried to spot the vixen through her binoculars. Then she saw the fox, struggling to move, her back leg spotted with blood. 'She's been hit!' she cried out.

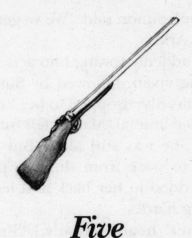

Five

Mandy was horrified. 'She's been shot. Look! Look at her back legs.'

Using only her forelegs, the vixen was dragging herself back to the earth. Dropping her catch, she was struggling to reach her cubs. As she got closer, Mandy could see the pain in the animal's eyes. The vixen stopped and looked around her. She was panting hard, trying desperately to gather strength. With a huge effort, she started forward again, taking three wobbly paces before dropping to the ground where she lay motionless. Mandy wanted to scream but no words would come out.

'Come on!' Simon said. 'We've got to get her to Animal Ark.'

Mandy suddenly sprang into action. She ran towards the vixen, followed by Simon, James and Michelle. She dropped to her knees beside the wounded animal. Mandy felt for a pulse in her neck. She was still alive! But blood was beginning to ooze from shotgun pellets that were embedded in her back and legs and she was panting hard.

'Hold her head, Mandy,' Simon said, whipping off his jacket. 'James, help me put this under her so I can keep her flat.'

Michelle moved a few paces away, pulled off her coat and waved it above her head. 'HOLD YOUR FIRE!' she yelled loudly, looking around frantically for the gunman. 'THERE ARE PEOPLE HERE!'

Tears ran down Mandy's cheeks and dripped on to the vixen's glossy red fur. 'She looks so small,' she said, her voice catching. 'She seemed so big and majestic on the moor.'

Just then heard voices coming towards them. Michelle called out a warning again.

'Oh no,' James groaned. 'Look who it is.'

Sam Western and Dennis Saville were approaching, shotguns hanging in the crook of their arms, a German shepherd dog trotting behind them.

'Quick, Simon, let's go,' Mandy urged. Simon had the vixen in his arms now. 'Don't let them see her.' Mandy ran alongside him.

'You stay here,' Simon said, turning to Mandy. 'Keep them away from the cubs.'

Mandy hesitated, torn between going with the vixen and staying to protect the cubs.

'I can manage,' Simon said firmly. 'I parked my car at the end of the track, it's not far.' Holding the fox in a gentle embrace, he strode away.

When Mandy turned and saw the men laughing and grinning, she felt her anger boil over. Screaming like a banshee, she ran at full speed up the moor towards the startled men. James glanced back at a cub peeping out of the earth, terrified. Then he was off, racing after Mandy.

'You . . . shot . . . a fox,' Mandy said, her breath coming in gasps. She managed to stop herself pummelling her fists on Sam Western's chest by jamming them into her pockets. 'You're not . . .' she took a deep breath, '. . . allowed to.'

'It's out of season,' James added, joining her. 'And this is common ground.'

Sam Western snorted. 'We've been shooting hares on my land and there's no season for that. I can't help it if a fox got in the way.'

'Do you realise you could have caused a very nasty accident, firing at random like that?' Michelle said, reaching them, her face thunderous.

'I wasn't firing at random. I aimed at the fox and I hit it,' Dennis Saville said proudly, stepping forward. 'Foxes are vermin,' he sneered. 'And anyway, that fox had a chicken in its mouth. Stolen from Blackheath Farm, I'll wager.'

'If that fox got into the chicken house it

probably killed half of Masters's hens tonight,' Sam Western agreed. 'Everyone knows foxes kill for the fun of it.'

'That's not fair!' Mandy blurted out. It was typical of Sam Western to say something like that. Wild animals killed because it was their instinct. It wasn't fair to blame foxes for being wild.

Sam Western eyed them suspiciously. 'Anyway, what are you doing out in the woods?' he demanded.

Mandy glanced at James. She knew he was thinking the same thing. If these two men found out about the cubs they would certainly kill them.

'We're bird-watching,' James announced quickly.

'A project for school,' Mandy added. 'Michelle's helping us.'

'Humph,' Sam Western snorted. 'Well, we're going to see Mr Masters now. And we'll see just what damage that fox *has* done. He'll be angry, *very* angry. You mark my words, we'll have a hunt in Welford before you can blink an eye.'

'And not before time,' Dennis Saville spat out over his shoulder as they left.

'What do we do now?' Mandy asked Michelle.

'We wait. And cross our fingers that the "helper" comes back. Hopefully, she'll take over the care of the cubs,' Michelle told them.

'Suppose she's too frightened to come back?' Mandy asked, worried that all the commotion might have scared her off.

'She won't be. Foxes live on the edge of fear all the time,' Michelle sighed. 'Being a wild animal is a tough business.'

They waited for most of the morning growing increasingly worried, but the little vixen didn't return.

'The cubs need food,' Mandy said. 'We could bring some with us tonight.' She looked anxiously at Michelle.

'It's more than that, Mandy.' Michelle pursed her lips. 'Food is important, of course, but the cubs will need the vixen to teach them how to fend for themselves.'

'What about the chicken the mother had in her mouth?' James said, suddenly 'It must still be there. We could find it and give it to the cubs.'

'Good idea, James,' Michelle agreed. 'You two go and find it while we finish packing up.'

Mandy and James backtracked through the wood and up to the moor. The picture of the injured fox was so strong in Mandy's mind that she couldn't remember where they had seen the vixen drop her catch. They searched in silence.

James found the chicken. They stared down at its soft white feathers.

'I know Mr Masters has to protect his chickens,' Mandy said sadly, 'but to her it *is* food, and she's such a good mother.' Mandy bent down and carefully picked up the chicken. 'She must have been really pleased to find this for her cubs.'

'Well, at least now we can make sure they get it,' James said. 'No wonder she had a job carrying it, it's enormous.'

They walked back to the earth. Not long ago it had been full of life and activity. Now it seemed sombre and still.

'Let's put the chicken right down in the entrance so the cubs don't have to come out for it,' James suggested.

Mandy nodded. 'I couldn't bear the thought of Sam Western and Dennis Saville coming back and finding the cubs,' she said with a grimace.

As they drove back to Animal Ark, Mandy was worried. What if the helper vixen had

raided the chicken farm too? Suppose Sam
Western saw her and shot her as well? She
glanced at the others. Michelle stared straight
ahead in silence. Janie wore an anxious frown.
Beside her, James's face was pale and worried.
Mandy wondered what was happening at the
surgery. What if the mother was so badly hurt
that she couldn't be put back with her cubs for
days? Mandy couldn't bear to think what might
happen to the cubs then.

Almost before Michelle had stopped the Jeep,
Mandy was out and running up the steps of
Animal Ark. 'Please let her not be too badly
hurt,' she begged silently. 'Please let her be all
right.'

Six

'Mum! Dad! How's the . . . ?' The door to the consulting room was open but Mandy faltered in the doorway at the sombre looks on her parents' faces.

'Mandy,' Emily Hope said, her face full of dismay. She put her hands on Mandy's shoulders. 'You're going to have to be brave, Mandy.'

'Is she badly hurt? I'll look after her,' Mandy hurried on. 'I know the rules about keeping wild animals, but Dennis Saville shot her on purpose.'

Mandy looked pleadingly at her father. 'Please, Dad, let me look after her. Just this once,' she begged.

Adam Hope looked stricken. 'Mandy, you know I would do anything I could to save an animal,' he said gently. 'But this time there wasn't anything we could do. She went into shock and died. I'm so sorry.'

'Dead! No, she can't be. She's got six cubs to look after!' Mandy could hardly take the news in. Slowly she realised that the proud little vixen, who had trusted them enough to let them film her cubs would never return to her earth. Mandy's dad came over and took her in his arms. Gratefully she fell against him and wept sad, bitter tears.

Eventually, Mandy's tears dried up. Guiltily, she realised that, up until now, she hadn't spared a thought for the others. She looked up and saw that Michelle and Janie were dabbing at their eyes and James was studying the floor.

'We did all we could, Mandy,' Michelle said softly.

'They'll *have* to rely on the helper now, won't they?' Mandy asked, her voice cracking.

Michelle nodded. 'I wanted to ask you about that,' she said to the Hopes. 'The young vixen is quite small. And we know that between the two foxes they hunted more than twenty times last night. I'm worried that the helper won't be able to manage on her own. What's your opinion?'

'I should think she'd wear herself out after the first week,' Emily Hope said honestly.

'I'll tell you what,' Adam Hope said, 'when are you going up to Piper's Wood again? I could come with you and see what condition she's in if you like.'

'That would be great. I'd like to go back tonight,' Michelle suggested. 'Do you feel up to it, Mandy?'

'Yes, I'm all right now,' Mandy said, nodding her head. 'It was just such a shock, I suppose I wasn't expecting it somehow.' She felt the tears begin to well up again and blinked several times.

'Then I suggest we meet you there,' Adam Hope suggested to Michelle. 'Why don't you all get a rest and then I'll bring Mandy and James up about sixish?'

'That suits me.' Michelle grimaced. 'Let's hope we have a happier outcome tonight.'

'I'd better go home and take Blackie out,' James said with a watery grin. 'Or he'll forget who I am.'

'I'll drop you off, James,' Adam Hope said. 'I've got to call in at High Cross Farm.'

'There's nothing wrong with Lydia's goats, is there, Dad?' Mandy said, alarmed.

'No, not really. It's just Houdini's got a grass seed in his eye and Lydia can't shift it.' Adam Hope hung up his white coat and collected his bag. 'You know what Houdini's like if he doesn't want to do something!'

Mandy and James grinned at each other. 'That goat is the stubbornest goat in the whole world,' said Mandy.

'Are you OK?' Emily Hope asked, as the Land-rover pulled out of the drive. She put an arm round Mandy's shoulders.

'Mum, do you think you ever get used to it?' Mandy asked softly. 'When an animal dies, I mean?'

'To tell you the truth, Mandy, no, I don't think you do.' Emily Hope ran her hands through her red hair and twisted it into a knot. 'Each one you lose is an individual.'

'But what about wild animals?' Mandy quizzed her. 'They're not pets and you hardly know them at all. Do you think it's silly to get upset?'

'Oh love, of course it's not,' Emily Hope reassured her. 'Dad and I were both terribly upset that we couldn't save the vixen. Wild animals are so brave and they have such dignity.

It's right to be sad. But then you have to let it go, and get on with helping the others, like the cubs.' She put the kettle on to make some tea. 'You must do the best you can for them, now.' She turned round and put her hands on her hips. 'Within reason, I mean.' She smiled gently but firmly. Mandy knew her mum meant that wild animals should never be reared as pets, as it would always put them at a disadvantage when they were returned to the wild.

'I know, Mum,' Mandy said. 'I feel better now.'

'And don't even think about toughening up where animals are concerned, Mandy Hope,' her mum said. 'After all, where would the animal population of Welford be without you?'

That evening when Mandy and James arrived at Piper's Wood with Adam Hope, they were surprised to see that Janie hadn't bothered to set up her camera.

'I've got a funny feeling about this earth. It's cold and quiet this evening,' Michelle explained. 'We've been here a while and there's been no activity whatsoever.'

'Do you think it's empty?' Mandy asked. 'That the cubs have strayed?'

'Yes, and I'm hoping that the helper vixen

has moved them.' Michelle replied. 'But we have to be prepared for the possibility that she didn't come back and they've wandered off looking for their mum.'

'I think I should take a look in the earth,' Adam Hope suggested. 'I can't stay too long, though, I've got to be back for evening surgery.'

Mandy clenched her fists and waited as her dad walked up to the earth. When he reached it, he crouched down and peered into the darkness. After a minute or so he stood up and beckoned the others.

'They've gone, I'm afraid,' he said dismally. 'I'm sure of it. The earth is silent and I'd expect to hear them mewing for their mother by now.'

'OK,' Michelle said. 'The cubs are too small to have gone very far. How long could they go without food, Adam?'

'Three or four days,' he told her.

'Look,' Mandy said, 'they've eaten the chicken.'

'Or something has,' James observed. On the patch of grass where the vixen had sat in the sunshine, only the carcase and a few feathers remained.

'So, what we should do is have a search around to see if we can find any sign of them,'

Michelle decided. 'We'll meet back here in half an hour.'

'OK. I'll look on the moors,' Adam Hope said, 'Michelle, if you and Janie check the woods, then Mandy and James can search the immediate vicinity.' Looking at Mandy he added, 'And don't forget how inquisitive foxes are. Check out even the most impossible-looking places.'

They started their search. Mandy got down on the ground and looked under the bramble bushes, James peered in holes in trees. Adam Hope searched on the moors and Michelle and Janie scoured the woods. Mandy grew more and more worried as the appointed time to meet up grew closer. As they made their way back to the earth, still looking desperately for the cubs, Mandy's head was buzzing with anxious thoughts.

'James, we *must* find them,' she burst out. 'They'll never survive on their own!'

'I don't know what else we can do,' James said miserably. 'Perhaps the others will have some news,' he added, trying to sound hopeful.

But Mandy felt that the chances of them finding the cubs were lessening.

'Nothing,' Michelle and Janie said when they arrived back.

'I'm afraid I didn't find anything either.' Adam Hope shrugged as he told them his news.

'Well, I think this means the young vixen must have come back and moved them.' Michelle sounded confident. 'She may have carried them one by one in her mouth to another earth.'

'So what are you planning to do now?' Adam Hope asked.

'Nothing, I'm afraid,' Michelle said glumly. 'We have to start again, I suppose, and find some more foxes. But what you could do, Mandy and James, is come up here some time tomorrow and see if there's any sign that the foxes have been back. I doubt they will have, but you never know.'

Mandy nodded vigorously. 'We'll do anything if it helps the cubs,' she told Michelle.

'Don't be too optimistic, Mandy,' Michelle said, seriously. 'Sometimes we never find out what happens to the animals we're watching.'

'Why don't we pop in at Bleakfell Hall on the way home?' Adam Hope suggested. 'You could ask Fox Watch to keep a special eye out for the cubs.'

'Thanks, Dad,' Mandy sighed. 'I've got to know what's happened to them.'

Mrs Ponsonby opened the door of Bleakfell Hall. 'Come in, do come in,' she said, her arms full of Pandora whilst Toby, dancing round her feet, did his best to trip her over.

'We can't stop, I'm afraid. I'm already late for surgery,' Mr Hope said in a purposeful voice. 'But we wondered if the Fox Watch volunteers could look out for a family of orphaned cubs? Six in all.'

'How utterly dreadful!' Mrs Ponsonby said, after Mandy had blurted out the full story. 'This is outrageous. Sam Western behaves as if all the countryside around here belongs to him.' Mrs Ponsonby popped Pandora on the floor and wrung her hands together. 'I'll phone everyone immediately. And, Mandy dear, I hope this doesn't mean the end of the film. I'm looking forward to helping with that.'

'Er, um . . .' Mandy was speechless.

'We'll let you know,' Adam Hope said, ushering Mandy and James back towards the Land-rover.

'That's all we need!' James muttered as they drove off.

* * *

Mandy and James had agreed to meet after breakfast the next day. Mandy had forced herself to eat a banana but she just wasn't hungry. Nothing could cheer her up. Although she had promised Michelle they would go and look at the earth, in her heart Mandy knew it would still be empty.

Now they were standing beside the deserted earth, Mandy scuffing the grass with the toe of her shoe. 'See that thin stick, over the entrance?' James asked.

Mandy looked. 'Yes, what about it? It's just a stick, isn't it?' she said irritably.

'Yes,' James said patiently, 'but I put it there last night. So we would know for sure if anything had visited the earth. It looks as if nothing has been near this place since we left,' he added with conviction.

'Oh, well done, James.' Mandy smiled briefly. She didn't tell him she didn't need a stick to know the earth was empty. She felt it, somehow.

'What should we do now?' James asked carefully.

'There's nothing much *to* do,' Mandy answered glumly.

James pushed his glasses up and down, then

shoved his hands deep in his pockets. 'We ought to start looking for another earth. We could go and ask Walter Pickard,' James suggested.

'Aah!' Mandy sucked in her breath. 'James, what shall we tell him? We promised to keep the earth a secret.'

'But it wasn't our fault,' James reminded her. 'We didn't lead Sam Western and Dennis Saville to the foxes. They were out shooting anyway.'

'James, let's leave Mr Pickard for the time being,' Mandy said. 'Why don't we go and see Mr Masters at Blackheath Farm and find out how many chickens he lost? The young vixen might have raided his farm too.' Mandy's mood had begun to lift now that she had something constructive to do. 'And we could go and see Libby.' Libby Masters was a few years younger than Mandy and James but they had become friends when her pet hen, Ronda, hatched out chicks.

'Race you up to the moor.' James shouted, as he scrambled on to his bike.

They were neck and neck when they reached the farm track that led to the Masters's farm, but James touched the gate first. 'I win!' he said jubilantly. 'Phew, it's windy up here.'

Mandy looked up. Puffs of white cloud sped across the sky.

The Masters's farm was high on the moor and they could see Welford village neatly laid out below them. Avoiding the potholes, Mandy and James rode down the farm track and into the farmyard. Mr Masters was at the door of the farmhouse, scraping mud off his wellington boots.

'Hello, Mandy, James. How are you both? Have you come to see Libby?' he asked. 'Her mum's taken her and Ryan into Walton.' Ryan was Libby's three-year-old brother.

'Actually, it was more you we wanted to speak to, Mr Masters,' Mandy said cautiously. 'About Sam Western.'

'And foxes,' James added nervously.

'Ah! Well you'd better come into the house,' Mr Masters said grimly.

Mr Masters took off his boots and went into the kitchen in his socks. Mandy and James wiped their feet on the mat and followed.

'Put the kettle on, Mandy, would you?' Mr Masters said. 'I'll just fetch my slippers. I'll have coffee but there's milk or juice in the fridge. Help yourselves.'

Mandy couldn't tell from Mr Masters's face what his reaction to them bringing up the subject of foxes was. He was just his usual, calm self.

It seemed an age to Mandy until they were sitting round the table with their drinks and a tin of shortbread. Eventually, Mr Masters sat down, took a breath and began talking. 'Sam Western and Dennis Saville did come to see me the other night,' he began, 'and they reckon most of the folk around here are itching to start a foxhunt.' Mandy tried to swallow the shortbread she was chewing but it wouldn't go down. Mr Masters continued. 'Western seems

to think that as I'm the only chicken farmer around here my agreement would swing it for him.'

'Oh, Mr Masters, won't you change your mind?' Mandy pleaded miserably. 'The vixen that Dennis Saville shot last night had six cubs, and she worked so hard to feed them. I know she stole a chicken but they had to eat.'

'Change my mind about what, Mandy?' Mr Masters said, looking bewildered.

'About agreeing to a foxhunt,' Mandy said, puzzled.

'I didn't agree, Mandy!' Mr Masters laughed. 'In fact, I sent him off with a flea in his ear.'

'You did?' James said, surprised. 'You don't mind foxes?'

'I like foxes, James.' Mr Masters bit on a piece of shortbread. 'A lot of chicken farmers do.'

'But how many chickens did she get from the hen-house?' Mandy rushed on. She was still puzzled by Mr Masters's attitude, but wanted to hear the whole story.

'None!' he replied mysteriously, grinning at their blank expressions. 'Let me tell you what happened.' He leaned back and took a few sips of tea. 'I was just shutting the hen-house yesterday evening when I got distracted by a hot-air balloon going over. Ryan, it seems, managed to open the door when I wasn't looking. Don't ask me how!' He threw up his hands. 'And *all* the hens got out. It was chaos.' He grinned at the memory. 'Anyway, eventually, I thought we'd caught them all, but obviously we must have missed one. *That's* the one the fox got.'

'So she didn't get into the hen-house at all?' Mandy smiled with relief.

'Nope,' said Mr Masters, smiling.

'We were worried that you might have lost loads of chickens.' James said.

'It does happen, James,' Mr Masters told them. 'If a fox gets into a hen-house it thinks, 'Wow, lots of easy food.' Its instinct is to kill more than it needs so it can bury some.'

'Isn't that called *caching*?' James asked. 'I've read about that.'

'That's right, James,' Mr Masters went on. 'It means that on a night when food is short, the fox can dig up the cached food.'

'But doesn't it go all mouldy?' Mandy screwed up her nose.

'Foxes aren't fussy about maggots, Mandy,' Mr Masters laughed. 'It's all food as far as they're concerned.'

'Yuck!' Mandy exclaimed.

'My problem is not with foxes at all. I pride myself on keeping my hen-house properly secure so that foxes *can't* get in.' Mr Masters immediately touched the wooden table and whistled. Mandy and James smiled at the old superstition. 'Foxes can break through chicken wire, so I've put weld-mesh wire on all my runs now, and at all my windows in the hen-houses. It's much stronger,' Mr Masters finished proudly.

'So that's why you're not bothered by foxes,' Mandy said.

Mr Masters nodded, then his face clouded over. 'My problem is rats. There seem to be so many at the moment and they *can* get in. They steal the eggs *and* kill the chicks. To tell the truth, I'd be happy if we had some foxes about the farm, to keep the numbers down. Most chicken farmers would.' He smiled. 'Very useful creatures, foxes.'

Mandy and James grinned in appreciation. It was all beginning to make sense.

'That's the other thing, Mr Masters.' Mandy suddenly remembered her worries. 'The six cubs have disappeared from the earth.'

Mr Masters ran a hand through his hair. 'If

the vixen didn't return they would probably have gone looking for her,' he said.

'But, well, there was another, younger vixen, a "helper", and we're hoping she's taken over the cubs. But, well, we just don't know where any of them are now.' Mandy's voice was full of anxiety as she thought of the cubs. 'If you see any foxes, will you let us know?'

'Of course I will,' Mr Masters said, getting up as the phone out in the hall began to ring. 'I'll keep my eyes peeled. But if they're not big enough to hunt for themselves,' he said, 'I wouldn't hold out too much hope for them, I'm afraid,' he finished quietly.

Seven

That night, Mandy lay in bed going over and over all the different things that might have happened. She couldn't get what Mr Masters had said out of her mind. Even as she drifted off to sleep, she could hear his words, 'If they're not big enough to hunt for themselves, I wouldn't hold out too much hope for them.'

What seemed like only minutes later, Mandy was jolted awake by the phone ringing. She tumbled out of bed and flew down the stairs. She glanced at the clock in the hall. It was seven o'clock already!

'Welford 703267, Animal Ark,' she answered politely.

'Mandy? Is that you, Mandy?' a quiet voice said on the other end. 'It's Libby Masters here.'

'Hi, Libby,' Mandy replied. 'Yes, it's me. Is something wrong with the chickens?'

'No!' Libby laughed. 'Nothing like that. It's just that Dad said that you would want to know straightaway, you know, about the foxes.'

Mandy's heart did a little nervous flip. 'Oh, Libby,' she swallowed hard. 'They haven't caused trouble, have they?'

'No, Mandy, it's *nice* news. I was woken up really early this morning by a strange noise, and when I looked out of my bedroom window there was a little fox, hunting about near the barn,' Libby told her happily. 'So I watched where it went and then when I took Ryan out for our daily farm walk before breakfast, I went to have a look.'

'Libby,' Mandy said in a trembling voice. 'Tell me, please, what did you find?'

'Some baby foxes!' Libby said excitedly.

Mandy was over the moon. 'Libby, you're a star!' she shouted. 'That's wonderful news. I'm on my way. Thanks.' Mandy hung up the receiver.

'What's wonderful news?' Adam Hope said, coming down the stairs in his dressing-gown.

'Libby's found the fox cubs, Dad!' Mandy did a little dance around him. 'Isn't that great?'

'Hold on a minute. How do you know they're *your* cubs?' her dad queried as he began making the tea. 'They could belong to another vixen.'

Mandy's doubt lasted for only a fraction of a second. 'They *are* my cubs,' she said emphatically. 'I just know it.'

'Far be it from me to question you.' Adam Hope gave her a lopsided grin. 'You seem to have a sixth sense where animals are concerned.'

'I'm going up there right away,' Mandy gabbled. 'I've just got to get dressed and phone Michelle and James . . . will you tell Mum the good news?'

When Mandy arrived at Blackheath Farm, Michelle and James were already in the farmyard, talking to Libby. 'I'm just telling Libby how grateful we are that she found the cubs for us,' Michelle told her, as she clambered off her bike and caught her breath.

Libby beamed. She was a friendly girl with pink cheeks and dark brown curly hair. 'I'll show you where the cubs are,' she offered.

Libby led them past the hen houses, round

the barn and across a field, to a spinney on the edge of the farmland. There she pointed past the trees to a small, derelict shed that had collapsed against a drystone wall. 'They're somewhere around there,' she announced.

'Let's wait quietly for them to come out,' Michelle said.

They settled under an oak tree on the edge of the spinney to wait. Mandy didn't take her eyes off the shed. James was just showing Libby his binoculars when the vixen came back, with two rats in her mouth.

Mandy felt a rush of excitement. 'It *is* the young vixen,' she breathed. 'You can't mistake her. Look at the dark fur round her eyes.'

The vixen slid through a gap and disappeared under the shed. Seconds later she emerged without the food and, finding a comfortable spot, curled up in the early morning sunshine.

'Look,' James whispered. 'Here come the cubs.' One by one the cubs emerged, their tummies fat and full of food.

'She's doing a good job, then,' Michelle observed.

Mandy was busy counting the cubs. She checked again. 'There's only five! One's missing,' she said, trying to keep the alarm out of her voice. 'You know, the one with the white ear tip.'

'Perhaps it's still down in the earth,' James suggested.

They waited and watched but the missing cub didn't surface.

'Mandy's right, I think,' Michelle said. 'It must be missing. There's no reason for one to stay behind in the earth. This *does* happen, you know. It's rare for *all* the cubs in a litter to survive.'

For a few moments they all stood silently watching the family of foxes. The vixen was trying to round up all the cubs but they wanted to play. As fast as she got one to the entrance of the earth the others chased off in the opposite direction. Eventually, she shepherded them all back under the shed. Then she gave a last look around and followed them down.

'She'll probably sleep all day now,' Michelle said softly. 'Listen, I've got to go to work but I suggest we come back and film for a couple of hours tonight. Is that all right with you two? I could pick you up at five.'

'We'll be ready,' Mandy and James promised.

'Now they've all gone into the earth, James and I could have a look for the lost cub,' Mandy offered.

Michelle looked doubtful. 'Well, OK, but

don't spend too long, Mandy. If the cub was anywhere near either this earth or the old one, the vixen would have found it.' She shrugged. 'But by all means have a look – you've nothing to lose.'

Mandy and James hunted through the spinney, then they walked all around the farmland but they didn't find the missing cub. Mandy knew she had to accept that the cub might have died. They cycled home, Mandy to help Simon with the lunch-time chores and James to take Blackie for a long-awaited walk.

'It's a shame,' Michelle said, when she came to pick them up later. 'But we've got five cubs and a vixen, which is a lot more than we had yesterday.' She grinned. 'I'd say this is turning into a success story.'

Once they had reached the farm and Janie was setting up the equipment, Michelle suggested that Mandy, James and Libby noted all the play items around the earth while they waited for the vixen to emerge.

'There's my yellow tennis ball!' Libby exclaimed softly, peering through Mandy's binoculars. 'I wondered where that had gone.'

'And that looks like a gardening glove,' James

noticed. 'The vixen *must* have been out today, they weren't there this morning.'

'You're right, James,' Michelle agreed.

'Look, here she comes,' Mandy said, tugging Michelle's sleeve.

Slowly the vixen came out from under the shed. She stretched and then trotted off on the first hunt of the night. Only minutes later, she returned with two rats in her mouth.

'She's so fast!' Mandy said, full of admiration for the little vixen.

'That will please your dad,' James whispered to Libby.

When the vixen took the food down to the cubs, she was welcomed by excited squeaking. But the next time she popped out from under the shed, the cubs tried to follow her. This became a routine – the fox cubs would eat inside the earth and follow the vixen out. No matter how much she shooed them down to safety, each time she set off they popped out again. It was perfect for the fox-watchers.

Libby put her hand over her mouth to stifle a giggle as three of the cubs had a tug of war with the gardening glove. The two other cubs barged into the threesome and they all tumbled over each other. A bit later, one found an old shoe and tried to drag it away before the others saw it.

'Too late,' Mandy said softly, as the other four charged after it, sinking their sharp, pointed teeth into the soft canvas. She was absolutely entranced. Within minutes the play became serious as each cub instinctively fought to possess the shoe. Soon, the spitting and snarling cubs had ripped it apart.

'They're very fierce for such little things, aren't they?' James said.

'It's only play-fighting,' Michelle said. 'But it's how they will learn to claim their portion of a vole or a rabbit.'

Mandy spotted the vixen coming through the trees. 'I wonder what she's got this time?'

Running to greet her, the cubs were wagging their tails and whimpering. The vixen dropped two items and the cubs pounced.

'That looks like a vole,' James said.

'But what's the other thing?' Michelle murmured.

As they watched, one of the cubs tossed the object into the air and the others pounced on it.

'Let me see,' said Libby. James let her look through the binoculars. 'Oh no,' she said in a worried voice.

'What's the matter?' Mandy asked.

Everyone looked at Libby. 'I know what that is,' she said, with a tremor in her voice. 'That's Ryan's favourite teddy bear. He lost it this morning.' Everyone looked back at the cubs. 'He won't go to sleep without it!'

'I'm afraid he'll have to,' Mandy said. 'Just look at it as Ryan's contribution to the cubs' education!' Everyone burst out laughing.

Mandy looked back at the vixen with her adopted cubs. This really was a perfect way to spend an evening.

'Thanks for the lift,' Mandy said, as Michelle dropped her home. She yawned as she walked up the drive. This was the third night she'd been up late watching the foxes at Blackheath Farm.

'And *I* say it most definitely was.' Mrs Ponsonby's voice rang out from Animal Ark's reception even though the door was closed.

Mandy looked at her watch. Evening surgery should have been over ages ago. What was Mrs Ponsonby doing here? Mandy pushed the door and her mouth dropped open. The reception was full of people. Her dad was standing behind the desk looking concerned as Mrs Ponsonby was lecturing the entire room.

'Everyone knows dogs like *that* chase and kill anything that moves,' she announced, glaring at the offending dogs. Her eyes flashed behind the pink glasses, and the brim of her hat wobbled furiously as she shook her head.

'I can assure you, madam,' said a tall thin man with long hair in a ponytail, and a gold earring in one ear, 'my dogs would never hurt anybody or anything. They are far too well-trained.'

The man was holding something wrapped in a shawl in his arms. The two 'dangerous' dogs sat perfectly still and well-behaved behind their master. Beside him stood two scruffy-looking children and a woman with short, spiky, maroon-coloured hair. Mandy was delighted to see them all. Jude Somers and his wife Rowan were travellers who helped out occasionally at the Spry sisters' place.

'Hi, everyone,' Mandy said from the doorway, just managing to make herself heard during a pause in the argument. Everyone turned to face her. She squatted down in the doorway and the two children ran over and threw their arms round her neck.

'Mandy, Mandy, we're back!' they squealed happily, as Mandy hugged them tight.

The sign on the wall reads:

SURGERY HOURS
M.. 9 - 10.30 4 - 6
Tu.. 9 - 10.30 4 - 6
W.. 9 - 10.30 4 - 6
Th.. 9 - 10.30
F.. 9 - 10.30 4 - 6
S.. 9 - 10
AFTERNOONS
BY APPOINTMENT

'So I can see,' Mandy grinned, holding them at arm's length. 'Skye, you've grown so tall!'

'And me, and me,' Jason said, standing on tiptoes and pushing his sister away. 'I'm tall too.'

Mandy stood up, Jason and Skye each holding one of her hands. 'What's happening here?' she asked, looking at her dad.

'I'll tell you, Mandy,' said Mrs Ponsonby, striding across the room. 'I found these . . . these . . . *people*, coming down the lane carrying a dead fox cub.' She paused and gestured at the bundle in Jude's arms. Mandy felt her face draining of blood. Mrs Ponsonby peered over her glasses at her. 'I thought you'd be shocked. Those wretched dogs are to blame.'

Jude and Rowan were silent. Each wore a look that said 'We've heard all this before.'

'Humph,' Mrs Ponsonby snorted. 'Wild, completely wild. The poor fox cub didn't stand a chance against those vicious animals.' She took out a hanky and blew her nose. 'No!' she declared solemnly. 'Fox cubs will never be safe with those dogs back in Welford.'

'Dad?' Mandy raised her eyebrows at her father.

'May I see the cub please, Jude?' he asked, coming out from behind the desk.

'Of course,' Jude replied. 'We were bringing it here when we were' – he gave a little cough – 'interrupted.'

Adam Hope took the bundle from Jude and looked at the cub. 'Well,' he said seriously, 'there's no question about it . . .'

Mrs Ponsonby smiled smugly to herself.

'Neither of those two dogs could possibly have killed this cub.' Mr Hope announced.

'WHAT?' Mrs Ponsonby demanded. 'What did you say? That can't possibly be right.'

'I said, neither of those dogs could have done it,' Mr Hope repeated. 'It's as simple as that.'

'But, but how?' Mrs Ponsonby spluttered. 'How do you know?'

'Although small dogs *can* be responsible for killing cubs, in this case, I can tell by the teeth marks that a much larger animal has taken this cub in its jaws and killed it,' Adam Hope explained. 'It must have been a big dog with a wide snout, at least as big as a German shepherd or a Labrador. Those dogs' snouts,' he nodded towards Spider and Joey, 'are far too narrow.' Mandy winced, thinking of Dennis Saville's dog. 'Also, Mrs Ponsonby, I happen to agree with Jude that his dogs are very well-trained.' Adam

Hope smiled kindly at Jude and Rowan. 'Did the dogs track the body down?'

Jude nodded.

Mrs Ponsonby visibly deflated. 'I don't know what to say,' she admitted, turning to face Jude and Rowan. 'I've made a dreadful mistake. How can you ever forgive me? Well, of course you can't!' She had made up her mind. 'What a fool I have made of myself.'

'Forget it!' Jude said graciously. 'It happens. We're used to it.'

'Forget it?' Mrs Ponsonby declared. 'I couldn't possibly forget it. I jumped to all the wrong conclusions and didn't stop to listen. I am very sorry.' Mrs Ponsonby was becoming agitated. She sat down heavily on a chair and began fanning herself with a folded-up handkerchief. Mandy looked pleadingly at Jude.

'Madam,' he said, 'please, it's no big deal. You said you're sorry, and we accept. Now let's just forget it.'

Mrs Ponsonby looked gratefully at Jude. She stood up and held out her hand. Jude gave a little bow and shook it.

'Sir,' Mrs Ponsonby declared, 'you are a true gentleman.'

Mandy crossed to the desk where Adam Hope

was holding the cub. 'Dad,' she asked softly, 'can I see?'

'Are you sure you want to, love?' her dad asked.

Mandy nodded and moved the shawl aside. She turned the little head and her heart sank. The tip of the ear was white. Mandy caught her breath. 'It's the cub that went missing,' she said.

FOXWATCH
FIGHTS for FOXES
Don't let
this horror
in Welford!

NAME   ADDRESS   SIGNED

Eight

Mandy quietly told the Somers family about the fox family, stroking the cub's ears as she spoke. 'Will you bury it with its mum, please, Dad?' she asked quietly.

'Of course, love,' her dad agreed. 'We'll do it tonight.'

Mrs Ponsonby wiped the corner of her eye with her hankie. 'Mandy, we *must* do something,' she insisted. 'This fox issue has to be sorted out once and for all. We can't have fox cubs being orphaned all over the place because of Sam Western.' She took a deep breath and stuck out her chest. 'A petition is what's needed,' she declared. 'Yes, and *everyone* will sign it, or I shall want to know why. You and James can take it around.'

'Yes, but . . .' Mandy began to explain that she and James were too busy, but Mrs Ponsonby interrupted.

'No buts, Mandy dear,' Mrs Ponsonby said. 'We'll clear this matter up and be done with it.' She put her hankie back in her handbag and shut it with a firm snap. 'I shall expect to see you at Bleakfell Hall first thing in the morning. Goodnight, everyone.'

By early the next morning Mandy had decided on a plan of action. 'James and I will go up to check on the cubs and the vixen as we arranged with Michelle,' she told her parents over breakfast. 'Then we'll call in on Mrs Ponsonby, get the petition and take it around the village. When we've done that, we'll come back and do my chores here and then . . .' Mandy paused to take a bite of toast.

'And when are you planning to breathe, Mandy?' Adam Hope asked, raising his eyebrows.

'After we've met up with Michelle this evening to do the filming.' Mandy finished, laughing.

Michelle was right, Mandy thought to herself as she cycled to meet James. It *was* turning into a success story. The vixen and the cubs were safe. She was glad she knew the fate of the lost cub and, although she felt sad about it, it was almost a relief to know it wasn't wandering around about to starve to death. At least Sam Western couldn't shoot the foxes on Mr Masters's land.

James was waiting outside his gate. 'Your dad just rang. Michelle and Janie have gone up to the farm already,' he said. 'Oh, and Michelle said that Mr Masters has seen the vixen going hunting during the day as well as at night.'

'Gosh, she won't be able to manage that for long,' Mandy said with a frown. 'She's got to get *some* sleep.'

The vixen was outside the earth when Mandy and James arrived, curled up asleep in a patch of sunlight. Her usually glossy coat was beginning to look dull and they could see the outline of her ribs.

'She's getting run down,' Mandy said, anxiously.

'Oh look, the cubs are coming out,' James observed. The little fox cubs trotted over to the vixen and began worrying her. Nibbling at her ears and chewing on her tail, they forced the vixen to wake up. She stood up to move away but the cubs followed her.

'They're hungry,' Michelle said. 'Although she's hunting almost constantly it's not providing enough food for them.'

The vixen began grooming the cubs, licking their ears and nuzzling at their feet. She herded them back to the earth and turned to set off hunting but as she turned her back they were out again, running after her. The vixen suddenly whirled around, causing the cubs to skid to a halt in a heap. Thumping the ground with their tails they lay on their sides with their ears flat against their heads.

'That's the submissive posture,' Michelle told them. 'It shows they know who's boss.'

The vixen led the cubs back to the earth again and this time they stayed put. She trotted off and was gone a long time, returning with a small rabbit in her jaws. The cubs rushed at her all at once, leaping on the kill, each one trying to claim it for itself. Off went the vixen again.

'At this rate she's going to wear herself out,' Michelle said, a note of concern in her voice.

'What can we do?' Mandy said, frowning. 'She's only been feeding them on her own for a few days. What will happen to her after a week?'

'We'll have to wait and see, Mandy,' Michelle said, thoughtfully. 'We'll come back again tonight.'

As they walked back to the farmyard, Mandy told Michelle and Janie about the cub Jude's dogs had found. She had already filled James in on the bike ride over. 'Anyway,' Mandy told them, 'now Mrs Ponsonby is going to start a petition.'

'That would be excellent, Mandy,' Michelle said. 'You can count on my name for a start.' She climbed into her Jeep.

'And me,' Janie added, going round to the passenger seat. 'See you later.'

When Mandy and James arrived at Bleakfell Hall, Mrs Ponsonby's car was just pulling up outside the house. 'Goodness me,' she puffed. Her face was as red as the poppies on her hat. 'I *have* been busy this morning. I went into Walton to the library to get the petition photocopied. Hold this for me please, James.' She lifted a box out of her car.

James nearly sank to his knees when he took

the weight of it. He gave Mandy a panicky
look.

'Come along, darlings!' Mrs Ponsonby said,
opening the back of the car. Toby jumped out
on to the drive, and Mrs Ponsonby lifted
Pandora down beside him. 'Come along,
children, inside.' The dogs rushed up to Mandy
and James, yapping round their feet.

Mandy grinned at James. 'Does she mean us
or the dogs?' she whispered.

James struggled with the heavy box. 'If this is
the petition, there are enough copies for the
whole village to have one each,' he said.

'Put the box on the table, please, James. It's

full of dog food,' Mrs Ponsonby ordered, taking off her coat, then putting on a vast apron and tying it behind her back. 'There, my precious,' she said to Pandora, who was trying to climb on to Mandy's lap. 'I'll get you a drinky in a moment.' She bustled around in the kitchen. 'Thank you, James. Now, rosehip tea or lemonade?'

'Are you asking us?' Mandy said with a smile.

'Of course, Mandy,' Mrs Ponsonby replied starchily. 'The dogs prefer water!'

'Lemonade, please,' Mandy and James said together.

'Now,' Mrs Ponsonby said, when they were seated at the table. 'Here's the petition.' She reached into a folder, pulled out a sheaf of papers and handed them a copy each. Mandy stared at the piece of paper. FOX WATCH FIGHTS FOR FOXES it said in big capital letters. There was a terrible picture of a pack of hounds killing a fox underneath, with *Don't Let This Happen In Welford!* emblazoned across it. Underneath were columns for people's names, addresses and signatures.

'What do you think?' Mrs Ponsonby asked eagerly, her eyes shining behind her glasses with their pink frames.

'It's very ... hard-hitting,' James said, struggling for words.

'All the more reason for people to sign then, isn't there?' Mrs Ponsonby said. 'You only get one chance with petitions.'

'You don't think it'll put people off?' Mandy asked carefully.

'No! Petitions have to get straight to the point,' Mrs Ponsonby retorted. 'Now, here are some for you to take back down to Welford with you.' She handed James a dozen copies and gave the same to Mandy. 'I've made some posters to go up in the shops, you two do the houses.'

Mandy and James sped off to petition the whole village house by house. By late afternoon Mrs Ponsonby had made sure that the village was covered with posters. They were posted on the windows of the Fox and Goose, with a note saying *Come in and sign*. Mrs McFarlane from the post office put up three on her notice-board, and had the petition on the counter. The oak tree had posters in plastic folders telling people where they could go to sign. There were two stuck up next to the village hall, and one by the church. Mandy and James arrived back at Animal Ark, tired but elated, their petitions covered with signatures.

'It's the picture that does it,' Mandy told her mum and dad. 'As soon as people saw the picture and realised how cruel hunting really is, they couldn't wait to sign.'

'And some kept the petition, so that members of their family who were at work could sign later,' James said. 'They promised to deliver them to the post office.'

'Can I put one on the notice-board, please?' Mandy asked her mum.

'Yes, of course,' Emily Hope said, signing her name on the bottom of James's form. 'Are you going back up to watch the foxes tonight?'

'Yep,' Mandy said, looking at her watch. 'And we should be going soon.'

'I've made you a plate of sandwiches to eat before you go,' Emily Hope said. 'And don't worry about your chores, good old Simon has already done them.'

'Brilliant, Mum, thanks,' Mandy said, giving her mum a hug.

'Thanks, Mrs Hope,' James called over his shoulder, as he followed Mandy through to the kitchen.

'Wow,' Mandy said. 'I didn't realise how hungry I was.' They'd finished the sandwiches and were smearing jam on some of Gran's scones which Emily Hope had left out for them.

'I hope you've saved one of those for me.' Adam Hope said, coming into the kitchen and taking a seat at the table. 'How's the film going?'

'There's a couple left in the tin,' Mandy said, 'and the film's going well. But I meant to ask you about the vixen. She isn't getting any rest. She spends all her time hunting.'

'She's really worn out,' James added, picking up the last crumb off his plate.

'Could we take her some food?' Mandy said. 'What do you think, Dad?'

'It would certainly help, but you'd need to be careful what you gave her,' Adam Hope said. 'People often leave out a bowl of dog or cat food, but in this situation you would need to leave food she can carry back to the cubs.'

'Like a chicken carcase?' James asked.

'Normally, I would say yes, James,' Mr Hope said, smiling, 'but I shouldn't think Mr Masters wants the foxes to get a taste for chicken. What does Michelle want to do?'

'Michelle wants the film to be as natural as possible,' James said. 'We're supposed to be observing and not interfering.'

'But man has already interfered by shooting

the mother vixen,' Mr Hope pointed out. 'In a way you're just redressing the balance. Michelle will know what to do.'

When they arrived at Blackheath Farm that night, Michelle was already waiting for them. 'Good, I'm glad you're here, we've got a problem,' she told them. 'Janie and I arrived quite early and we've been watching the cubs. And I'm certain another one has gone missing.'

Mandy fought to keep the panic from rising inside her. 'Quick, let's look for it before it gets dark!' she said, urgently.

'Where shall we start? It could be anywhere,' James said. 'Still, at least Mr Masters's dog is too well-trained to have taken it.'

'James! That's it!' Mandy exclaimed. She looked at Michelle. 'James has just given me an idea. Why don't we ask Jude to bring Joey and Spider? They'll find it easily enough.'

'Can we get hold of him?' Michelle asked, taking her mobile phone out of her bag. 'Has he got a phone?'

'We can ask the Sprys to give him a message,' Mandy said, thinking on her feet. 'The camper van is parked up there. He could get over here really quickly.'

'OK, Mandy, you call the Sprys.' Michelle

handed her the phone. 'I'll just go and tell Mr Masters what we're doing.'

Mandy dialled the number but the Sprys' phone just rang and rang.

'They don't always answer it, you know,' James told her.

'Well, they'll have to. I'm not giving up,' Mandy hissed between her teeth.

Miss Marjorie answered eventually on the twelfth ring. Mandy poured out their request.

'I'll go right away, Mandy,' Miss Marjorie said, hanging up.

Mandy and James found Michelle in the farmyard and told her they'd got through, then walked up the track to wait for Jude. Tense with worry, Mandy paced up and down, as minutes seemed to take hours to pass.

'Here he comes!' James exclaimed, peering through his binoculars across the fields to the road. 'I didn't recognise the van, he's painted it in some sort of pattern.'

The battered old red van that the family lived in came chugging up the track.

'It's the fox posters,' James said, as it drew closer. 'Jude's covered the van with our posters.'

The van pulled into the farmyard and the back door opened. Rowan and the children got out. Spider and Joey sat in the back, waiting.

'Right,' Jude said, getting out of the driver's seat. 'First I'd like to look at the earth and decide where I think it's best to start.' Calling the dogs he set off with Mandy and James, while Michelle talked to Rowan and the children.

'As likely as not, the cub's in that spinney,' Jude pointed. 'We'll start on the far side and work our way toward the earth.'

Dusk was just beginning to fall and shadowy shapes in the wood began to merge. Jude worked the dogs in ever decreasing circles. Several times they surprised rabbits, but there was no sign of the fox cub.

Mandy was beginning to lose hope. It wasn't looking good. But then, suddenly, Spider veered away to the right, his nose on the ground, sniffing as he went. Soon Joey joined him and Jude loped along behind them. Mandy followed, with James hot on her heels, fear shooting through her at the thought of what the dogs might find.

They were at the other side of the wood now, following the drystone wall that marked the boundary of Mr Masters's land. Joey and Spider stopped at a place where the wall had collapsed. They looked expectantly up at Jude, their tails wagging. Mandy and James were out of breath as they caught up. Jude put a finger to his lips and then cupped his hand behind his ear to listen.

Mandy concentrated hard, but all she could hear was her heart pounding and the blood rushing in her head.

Then she heard it, a faint mewing. It was coming from underneath the pile of heavy stones where the wall had fallen down. 'The wall's fallen on it!' she cried in alarm.

Nine

'We've got to get it out,' Mandy said, collapsing on her knees in front of the wall.

Jude and James hurried to join her. With their bare hands they began digging frantically at the loose stones. Mandy worked hard, not wanting to think about the injuries the cub might have sustained, buried under all this rubble.

Suddenly, Jude stopped digging and stood up.

'What is it?' Mandy asked.

Jude grinned. 'I think if we move this big flat stone, we'll find the cub,' he said, 'I'm beginning to think it crawled in underneath here,' he pointed to an opening, 'and dislodged a stone that trapped it inside. I don't think the wall fell on it at all.'

'Oh, I hope you're right, Jude,' Mandy said, crossing her fingers while he pulled away the stone. Sure enough, as they watched, the cub wriggled out. Mandy was itching to help it, but Jude put a hand out to stop her.

'Don't touch it!' he said. 'You'll transfer your smell to it. Now it's free, the vixen will find it soon enough.'

When Mandy and James reached the farm-yard, Michelle was just coming back with Rowan and the children. 'We saw the foxes, we saw the foxes,' Skye sang to Mandy and James.

'They were having their dinner,' Jason told them.

Michelle didn't need to ask Mandy if they had been successful, she could tell by their smiling faces. 'Oh, well done, dogs,' she said, bending down to stroke their brindled coats.

'We'd never have found the cub without them,' Mandy told her proudly. Then she asked, 'How's the vixen?'

'She's very tired, but just about coping, I think,' Michelle said. 'She hasn't been back since the cub went missing, though.' Jude said he had to go, so they all waved him and his family off as they drove back down the track, then they returned to watch the foxes.

Mandy and James had just crept back to their watching place near the earth, when the vixen returned. She dropped a vole by the waiting cubs, then ran inside the earth. Almost immediately she shot out and gave a warning cough. Instantly, the cubs dived for the safety of the earth.

'Do you think she knows the cub's missing?' James asked.

'Course she does!' Mandy said. 'She knows how many cubs she's looking after.'

With a loud bark the vixen made off into the spinney.

'I bet she comes back with the cub,' James said.

'Dad said it wouldn't hurt to give the vixen some food,' Mandy told Michelle as they waited. 'If you don't mind, that is.'

'I've been thinking the same thing, Mandy,' Michelle said thoughtfully. 'I don't want to interfere, but . . .'

'We've got action, guys!' Janie announced.

Mandy looked through her binoculars, hardly daring to hope that James had been right. Relief flooded through her as she saw the vixen trotting back, with the runaway cub held gently by the scruff of its neck in her mouth. 'She's found it,' she breathed.

'You'll have to help Mrs Ponsonby, Mandy,' Emily Hope said next morning as she put the breakfast things on the table. 'She's gone to such a lot of trouble. All you have to do is collect up the petitions from the various notice-boards in the village.'

'James and I had planned to spend all day watching the foxes.' Mandy groaned, flopping in a chair. 'We wanted to make a note of how many times the vixen hunts during the day. It's important.'

'And so is Mrs Ponsonby's petition,' her mum said. 'This might be your best chance to stop Sam Western in his tracks. I've heard she's got a huge convoy of people coming to lend support.'

'I know you're right,' Mandy said, wrinkling her nose. 'It's just that I love watching the cubs. What time is she coming?'

'At one o'clock,' Emily Hope said, glancing at the clock. 'That should give you enough time.'

'Right,' Mandy agreed. 'I'll call James and tell him.'

Mandy walked down to the village. She had arranged to meet James outside the post office without their bikes, to give Blackie a walk. Her mum was right as usual. It would be brilliant if the petition stopped Sam Western's hunt plans.

Mandy and James quickly collected up all the petitions. They were astonished at the number of names that had been signed.

In the post office, Mrs McFarlane, the postmistress, took the petitions from the board while Mandy and James were choosing crisps. 'Here we are,' she said. 'And best of luck!'

'Let's sit on the bench outside the Fox and Goose and look at these while we're eating our crisps,' James suggested.

'I didn't think there *were* so many people in Welford,' Mandy said, slipping her foot out of her shoe and tickling Blackie's tummy with her toes. 'Look, James,' she said passing him a petition form. 'Lydia Fawcett's signed, and look!' Mandy's mouth fell open. She could hardly believe it. 'Mr Parker-Smythe has as well.'

'Wow,' James said, opening his crisps. 'And he lives right next door to Sam Western!'

'Let's see if the Gills have signed.' Mandy flicked through some petitions. 'Their place is nearby, too,' she said, crunching on a cheese and onion crisp. 'Nope, can't find them.'

'Never mind, what we've got is very impressive,' James said. 'Sam Western can't ignore this, especially if your mum's right and lots of people turn up as well.'

'They're all meeting up at Animal Ark at one o'clock,' Mandy said checking her watch.

James nodded, reading another form. 'Here's Walter Pickard's name.'

'Someone talking about me?' a familiar voice said behind them.

'Hello, Mr Pickard,' Mandy said. 'We just found your name on the petition.'

'Aye, it's there all right,' Walter said. 'Along wi' all the others.' He shook his head and sucked his teeth. 'That were a bad do up at Piper's Wood.' He looked from Mandy to James. 'Make sure that Sam Western knows we don't want any more foxes *mistaken* for hares!'

'We will,' Mandy promised. 'But aren't you coming?' she asked, disappointment in her voice. Walter Pickard would be a good person to have along when they faced Sam Western, because of all his special knowledge of the countryside.

'I had planned to, young Mandy, but my grandson Tommy is feeling a bit peaky.' He bent and scratched Blackie between the ears. 'I promised I'd go and stay with him while his mum goes out.'

'That's a shame,' Mandy said. 'I hope Tommy feels better soon. Tell him all about the fox cubs, won't you?'

'I will that,' Walter promised. 'Welford Cubs were right proud when they had Lucky as a mascot. Tommy's always interested to hear about foxes.' Walter put his cap on and walked away.

'I was thinking,' Emily Hope said. 'Why don't you get Mrs Ponsonby to drop you at Blackheath Farm on the way back from delivering the petition?' Mandy and James had gone back to Animal Ark for lunch and were tucking into cheese-on-toast.

'Good idea,' Mandy said. 'At least we'd have the afternoon to watch the foxes that way.'

'And Michelle's doing the last bit of filming tonight,' James said, cleaning his plate.

'Seconds, James?' Mrs Hope asked. 'You'll need to keep your strength up today.' She grinned.

'Please.' James pushed his plate forward. 'It's delicious.'

At a quarter to one Mrs Ponsonby arrived in

her car. She was wearing a pale-green flowered dress and her freshly curled hair was covered by a straw hat weighed down with mauve and pink artificial busy Lizzies.

Mandy had to bite her cheek to stop herself from laughing.

'She looks like she's going ballroom dancing,' Adam Hope muttered behind them. 'Not leading a protest.'

'Adam!' Emily Hope nudged him with her elbow.

'Nobody here yet?' Mrs Ponsonby said, looking around her. 'I do hope we'll have enough cars to carry everyone.'

Just then, Jean came out from reception with a message. 'I'm afraid your regulars from Fox Watch won't be here,' she said to Mrs Ponsonby. 'They were coming together in one car and they've just phoned to say they've broken down.'

'Oh dear, that's too, too bad,' Mrs Ponsonby said with a sigh. 'Ernie Bell stopped me in the village. He's got an appointment at the opticians in Walton, so he won't be joining us either.'

'And we met Walter Pickard this morning,' Mandy remembered. 'He's got to look after his grandson.'

'Where *is* everybody else?' Mrs Ponsonby

looked at her watch. 'It's nearly one o'clock.'

'Who else are you expecting?' Adam Hope asked.

'Well,' Mrs Ponsonby floundered a bit. '*Everyone* who signed my petition promised they'd come.' She looked at the Hopes. 'Will we have *your* support?'

Adam Hope coughed. 'Much as I'd like to come . . .' he said. Mandy looked up at him. '. . . duty calls in the form of an Afghan hound in Walton with kidney failure.'

'And I've got afternoon surgery,' Emily Hope smiled apologetically.

'Michelle said she and Janie wanted to come, but they've got too much editing to do,' Mandy said. 'The programme's important too.'

'Well, Mandy and James,' Mrs Ponsonby decreed. 'It looks like saving the foxes of Welford is completely down to us three. Come along.' She opened the car doors and waited for them to get in. 'Let battle commence!'

Mandy and James exchanged glances. *Some protest this is going to be*, Mandy thought nervously to herself.

'I bet Sam Western won't take a bit of notice of us,' James whispered to Mandy behind his hand.

'Wait and see, James,' Mrs Ponsonby said, overhearing. 'It is quality, not quantity that counts. We can be just as forceful as a big deputation.' She adjusted her hat in the rear-view mirror and then set off. 'After all, we feel *very* strongly about this. We just have to put that across to Mr Western.'

When they reached the entrance to Upper Welford Hall, James jumped out to open the gate.

'I have to admit I admire his gardens,' Mrs Ponsonby said, looking around as she drove up the drive. 'It's a gardener's paradise. Every plant behaves itself perfectly. These roses wouldn't *dare* grow suckers.' She leaned back and said conspiratorially. 'I *have* heard that they even vacuum the paths.'

Mandy and James stifled giggles. Mrs Ponsonby was always inclined to believe gossip, however unlikely it seemed.

'I prefer your gardens, Mrs Ponsonby,' Mandy reassured her. 'At least they look more, more . . .' She looked to James for help.

'More *natural*,' James said. 'More lived in.'

'Thank you, dears. With two dogs like mine what else can they be?' She parked the car opposite the house and they all got out. The

Hall had an old-fashioned bell-pull and Mrs Ponsonby gave it such a hard tug they could hear it jangling through the house.

Dennis Saville came from round the side of the house and stood at the bottom of the steps watching them.

'This concerns you too,' Mrs Ponsonby called down to him. 'Come along.'

Reluctantly Dennis Saville climbed the steps. 'I'm a busy man,' he said, glaring from Mandy and James to Mrs Ponsonby.

Mrs Ponsonby pulled the bell-pull again. Moments later, the door flew open and Sam Western stood there. 'What on earth is going on?' he shouted angrily. 'They must have heard that in Walton.'

'Don't be silly, Mr Western,' Mrs Ponsonby said lightly. She drew herself up and declared in a loud voice, 'We, from Welford Fox Watch, summon you to take notice of this petition.' She turned to Mandy and James and urged them forward with a nod of her head. They both entered into the spirit of things by solemnly holding out their armfuls of paper. 'Duly signed by virtually every person in this village and its outlying districts,' Mrs Ponsonby continued.

'Huh!' Sam Western snorted. 'So where *are* they all, these *concerned* people, then?'

Mandy had had a horrible feeling he was going to ask that. She looked at James and he gave a little grimace.

'MR WESTERN,' Mrs Ponsonby's voice was as cold and hard as steel. 'The three of us, and a few other people, *know* what happened up at Piper's Wood the other morning.' She paused to let the message sink in.

'I didn't do anything wrong,' Sam Western said. 'I was shooting hares, *that's* legal.'

But Mandy thought he looked a bit nervous now.

'We know that a fox *was* shot, *on* common land *and* out of season.' Mrs Ponsonby was in full swing now. 'Mandy, James and I chose, yes chose, out of the goodness of our hearts to come alone. We chose not to embarrass you in front of all your business associates, and indeed, the whole of Welford.'

'And its outlying districts,' Mandy added. *Good old Mrs Ponsonby!* she thought. James nodded vigorously.

Mrs Ponsonby delivered her ultimatum. 'Now, either you give up this idea of a foxhunt or I shall take this whole matter one step further.'

'And you've got to promise not to shoot any more foxes,' Mandy said, warming to the subject.

Sam Western looked at the pile of petition sheets. Then he looked at Mrs Ponsonby. Lastly he looked at Mandy and James. He sighed. 'You're nothing but trouble, you two kids,' he said in a resigned voice.

Dennis Saville's face was beetroot red. Mandy felt a shiver down her back as he glared at her and James. 'Take no notice of these two, Boss . . . ' he began, stepping forward.

But Mrs Ponsonby interrupted him. 'Make up your mind, Mr Western!'

Mandy's heart was beating rapidly. She had to stay calm. She clutched the petition with an iron grip to stop her hands from shaking.

Sam Western gave another loud sigh. 'All right. I'll stop my plans for a hunt. But for this season only.' He narrowed his eyes at them. 'And if I find that foxes have bred in vast numbers and are causing trouble then I'll have to think again.'

'What about shooting foxes?' Mandy asked. It was no good stopping the hunt if he and Dennis Saville were still going to shoot them. 'You have to agree to stop that too.'

Mr Western looked weary. 'That too.'

'What about him?' James indicated Dennis Saville who was standing by with a look of open-mouthed disbelief on his face.

'He works for me. *I* give the orders round here,' Sam Western said sternly.

Mrs Ponsonby was satisfied. She looked at Mandy and James. They nodded. 'Then we'll just need your word on it, Mr Western,' she said sweetly.

'Good Lord, what are you on about, woman? Don't you trust me?' Sam Western spluttered furiously.

'Don't you "woman" me, Sam Western.' Mrs Ponsonby glared at him. 'And the answer to your question is no, I don't!'

'I give you my word. Are you happy now?' Sam Western said through clenched teeth.

'Not quite,' Mrs Ponsonby said, tapping her chin with a finger. 'I will expect confirmation of your resolve in writing, please.'

'Bah, you drive a hard bargain, woman,' Sam Western said, his face flushing. 'You'll have a letter from me in the next couple of days. *Now* are you happy?'

'Perfectly happy now, Mr Western.' Mrs Ponsonby gave him a smile. 'Perfectly.' She turned to Mandy and James. 'That's that then,' she said, giving them a broad wink. 'Goodbye, Mr Western, and don't forget now, or I will have to visit you again.'

Mrs Ponsonby ushered them down the steps towards the car.

James did a small running jump and punched the air. 'Yes!' Mandy exclaimed. 'We really did it!'

Ten

'Mrs Ponsonby,' Mandy said, with a note of awe in her voice. 'You were fantastic!'

'Well, thank you, my dear,' Mrs Ponsonby replied. Mandy saw her satisfied smile. 'I must admit I *am* feeling rather pleased with myself,' she said, slowing down behind a tractor. 'I will *not* be bullied, nor will I let the people of Welford be bullied!'

James elbowed Mandy in the ribs. But Mandy didn't care how over-the-top Mrs Ponsonby was today. 'Or the foxes of Welford,' she added happily.

'I didn't think just the three of us could convince Mr Western,' James said, joining in.

'Sam Western knows when he's beaten,' Mrs Ponsonby replied, nodding sagely. 'But I couldn't have done it without you two to support me.' She glanced at them quickly over her shoulder. 'You know, most of the local farmers signed our petition.'

'It's *so* brilliant that foxes will be safe around Welford now,' Mandy burst out.

'But we mustn't let up!' Mrs Ponsonby said. 'You heard what Sam Western said. It's only for this season.' She slowed down as she neared Blackheath Farm. 'We've got to keep the support up and do everything we can to keep the farmers on our side.'

'Mr Masters is already on our side,' Mandy told her.

'And Lydia Fawcett,' James added.

'If you could drop us here, that would be great,' Mandy said, as they approached the gate to Blackheath Farm.

'Right,' Mrs Ponsonby said, looking at her watch. 'I really must get back to the dogs. They'll wonder where I am. Shall I ring your parents and tell them the good news?'

'Yes, please,' Mandy said gratefully, getting out of the car.

She and James waved as Mrs Ponsonby drove

away. 'She *was* pretty impressive, wasn't she?' James said, setting off down the track.

Mandy nodded. 'It's like Mum and Dad said, there's a lot of huff and puff but she *does* get things done.' She laughed out loud. 'Did you see Dennis Saville's face?'

James grinned. 'I thought he was going to explode.'

'Now, we just want the little vixen to be coping,' Mandy said, as they crossed the field to the spinney, 'and everything will be great.'

When they reached the earth there wasn't a fox to be seen. 'She could be out hunting,' Mandy suggested. 'Or perhaps the cubs are letting her sleep more now. Let's sit under that oak tree and wait,' she said.

Mandy and James watched and waited. By late afternoon they were both feeling worried. The little vixen hadn't been out once.

'James, what do you think has happened?' Mandy said anxiously. 'Yesterday she was in and out all day.'

James nodded glumly. 'I know.' He thought for a few moments. 'But there could be lots of reasons.'

'Such as?' Mandy asked, her eyes bright with concern.

'Well,' he began, then paused.

'Tell me, James, I have to know,' Mandy said, sensing that he didn't want to upset her.

'Sometimes,' James began, 'vixens go away from their cubs to rest up somewhere else, to get a bit of peace and quiet. They just come back to feed them and play with them.'

'I don't think our little vixen would do that,' Mandy said. 'She's been too good a mother so far. And wouldn't the cubs be out calling for her?' She wasn't convinced.

'That's true,' James agreed. 'You know, she could have gone out and . . .' he looked at Mandy, '. . . not come back for a reason.'

Mandy thought about this for a moment. It would be too dreadful if something had happened to the little vixen. 'But surely the cubs would be out, wouldn't they, if she hadn't come back?' Mandy said. 'Maybe she's moved them again?'

James frowned. 'Or maybe she's in the earth and is just too exhausted to hunt any more!' he said.

'It's awful not knowing,' Mandy said in a small voice. 'I don't think I could bear it if we lost them now.'

'Perhaps Michelle will have some ideas,'

James said, trying to cheer her up. 'She and Janie should be here soon.'

But when they did arrive, Michelle seemed just as concerned as Mandy and James. 'I have to admit, I have been concerned about her wearing herself out,' she said. 'It's a terrific amount of work for a single vixen. Five hungry cubs.'

'Wait!' Janie said. 'She's coming out.'

Through her binoculars Mandy saw the little vixen coming out of the earth. Ears flicking she sniffed the wind, then trotted jauntily off to hunt. She didn't seem tired at all. She seemed positively perky.

'What *is* going on?' Michelle said softly. 'There's obviously nothing wrong with her at all. She must have got some rest.'

'But if she hasn't been hunting all day, why aren't the cubs hungry?' Mandy asked, feeling mystified.

'Look!' James said, under his breath. 'Another fox.'

Mandy felt a fizz of excitement go through the group as they saw an unfamiliar fox appear at the scene. As the fox drew nearer to the earth they could see it had a rabbit in its mouth.

'She's getting help from another vixen,'

Michelle said, with rising excitement in her voice. '*That*'s the answer.'

The fox took the rabbit into the earth and stayed down. After a few minutes she came out with the cubs following behind her. She picked up the gardening glove that was lying nearby and tossed it into the air. They all pounced on it, embarking on an energetic playfight.

But Mandy was only half watching the cubs' antics. She'd noticed something else.

'What is it, Mandy?' said Michelle. Mandy's eyes were wide and she was holding her binoculars with trembling hands. 'What's wrong?'

'Nothing's wrong!' Mandy said. 'But look at the cubs.' She waited while they looked. 'There's *six* cubs now and one is quite a bit bigger than the rest. You wait, when they stop jumping about you'll see.'

'Good gracious!' Michelle declared. 'You're right Mandy. I hadn't counted.'

Mandy was so excited now she could hardly keep still. 'Look, James, look at the new cub,' she blurted it out. 'Don't you recognise it?'

'It can't be, can it? It is! It's Lucky, I'm sure of it.' James was grinning widely.

'Mandy, look through the camera,' Janie said,

bending to be shoulder height to her. 'The foxes will be much clearer.'

Mandy looked through the viewfinder. For a few seconds she couldn't work out what she was seeing. Then slowly the scene came into focus. There was the bigger cub and as she watched, he turned and looked right at her. It was definitely Lucky. She recognised the way he put his head on one side when his ears pricked up.

Janie took over the camera to carry on filming, obviously delighted by the new, surprising twist in their film.

'But how has this happened?' Mandy asked Michelle, once she'd got over the surprise.

Keeping her voice as low as possible Michelle explained, 'I think that this vixen is the little vixen's grandmother.'

'So would the vixen that Sam Western shot have been Lucky's mum's daughter?' Mandy asked, catching on.

'That's right,' Michelle agreed. 'She would have been born three years ago, and Lucky's mum obviously let her daughter take over half her territory. The daughter had the young vixen last year, and she stayed to help with these cubs this year. That's often what happens in fox families.' She tapped her chin with her finger and smiled. 'I see now, this also solves another problem I had.'

'What was that?' James asked, keeping his eyes on the cubs.

'Well, I really didn't think we'd see Lucky and his mother around here.' Michelle explained. 'Normally, if you remove a fox from its territory, as you did with Lucky's mum when she was injured, within about four days another will have taken it over, and then the first fox will be driven off. So although you let Lucky and his mum loose on their original territory, I very much doubted we'd see them again.'

'But because Lucky's mum shares the territory with her daughter, there wasn't any problem,' Mandy guessed.

'Right,' Michelle agreed. 'What has happened here – and I'd stake my reputation on it – is that Lucky's mum came across the little vixen and the cubs, realised that she couldn't cope and decided to pool the litters and rear them together.'

'With two vixens hunting there shouldn't be a problem, should there?' James asked.

'No, there shouldn't. Lucky's mum will also be much more experienced at hunting and she'll know this territory like the back of her hand,' she said. 'Or should I say paw!'

Mandy and James laughed. Janie was too absorbed in her filming to hear.

'What would have happened if, say, Lucky's mum wasn't related to the little vixen?' Mandy wondered. 'And she found the cubs on her territory then?'

'She'd probably have killed them and driven the young vixen away,' Michelle said seriously. 'She's the dominant vixen on this territory and she wouldn't let an intruder in.'

'The young vixen is coming back,' Janie said, turning her head slightly, but keeping the camera on her shoulder perfectly still.

They all watched in silence as the young vixen took her catch down into the earth. The cubs followed her down immediately. Lucky's mum herded the last one in and then followed them down.

'Isn't it amazing to see the co-operation?' Michelle said. 'This is an excellent result. We couldn't possibly have wished for anything better.'

Mandy grinned. She couldn't agree more whole-heartedly.

A short time later in the fading light of dusk, both vixens came out of the earth with the cubs.

The two adults groomed the young foxes one after another. Mandy could see how much more foxy Lucky's face was now than the smaller, younger cubs whose faces were just beginning to lose their puppy look. She sighed happily.

'I think we have enough footage now, if you two can prise yourselves away,' Michelle said, interrupting Mandy's thoughts. 'I'd like to go back to Animal Ark and do a couple of pieces to camera, including a little piece about how you found Lucky.'

'Then we can get back to the studio and finish off the editing,' Janie said, turning off the camera.

Mandy and James took one last long look at the foxes.

'The cubs seem really safe now, don't they, James?' She looked at her friend who had a huge grin on his face.

They trooped back to the farmhouse and told everybody there the good news.

'I've already noticed a difference,' said Mr Masters, beaming at them. 'I haven't lost nearly so many eggs recently. Let's hope they keep up the good work. By the way, how did the petition go?'

Mandy and James looked at each other. They

could hardly believe it. In all the excitement with the foxes, they had both completely forgotten the petition.

'It's brilliant news,' Mandy told them. 'Sam Western promised *not* to start up a hunt and *not* to shoot any more foxes.'

'I'd say you two have had a pretty successful day,' Michelle said. 'And I think the fox population of Welford has a lot to thank you for!'

Eleven

Janie set the camera up in the garden at Animal Ark, while Michelle gave Mandy some pointers. James had insisted that Mandy should be interviewed alone, as he got embarrassed easily.

'Just look at the camera and speak naturally,' Michelle was saying. 'Talk about how you found Lucky in that dreadful trap, and then how you set him and his mother free after you had hand-reared him.'

Adam and Emily Hope were on the patio listening, and Jean and Simon stood at the back door of the surgery. On the third attempt all Mandy's nerves disappeared and she told the story perfectly without any hesitations.

'Mrs Ponsonby rang and told us all about the petition,' Mandy's dad said later, when they were sitting at the table eating supper. Michelle and Janie had dashed off to work on the film but James had stayed. 'We're very proud of you both. Mum and I think you've done a terrific job, both with the petition and with the film.'

'Michelle says it will be on early next week.' Mandy said. 'It's a shame the Spry sisters and Jude and Rowan won't be able to watch it.'

'We plan to record it anyway, but why don't we invite them here to see it?' Emily Hope said. 'It will be a bit of a squash but I should think they'd enjoy it nevertheless.'

'Mum, that's a great idea.' Mandy jumped up and gave her mum a hug. 'James and I will go over in the morning and ask them.' She looked at James.

'Fine,' James said. 'But please, Mandy, not *too* early.'

It was late when Mandy woke up the next morning. She went downstairs in her dressing-gown and phoned James. 'I'll meet you in about half an hour at the post office and we can go over to the Sprys'.'

'OK,' James answered. 'I'll bring Blackie. He's very cross that we've been out so much without him.'

'Tell him we'll make it up to him today,' Mandy said, laughing. 'Let's take him up on the moor for a really long run.'

Mandy got dressed and popped into Animal Ark to tell her parents her plans.

'So, have you come back to work at last, Mandy?' Simon teased, as he was cutting a guinea-pig's claws.

'Tomorrow!' Mandy said. 'Definitely tomorrow. I just want to go up and spend one last day with the foxes. Is that OK?

Simon nodded. 'Of course, you deserve it after your hard work.'

Jude was mowing the lawn in front of the house when Mandy and James arrived at the Riddings. He turned off the mower and came over to see them. 'How are the foxes?' he asked, jumping down from the little wall on to the drive. 'All present and correct?'

'Better than that,' Mandy said, going on to tell him all about the pooling of the litters.

Jude walked up to the house with them. Rowan, who had waved to them through the window, opened the door with a duster in her hand.

'Hi,' she greeted them with a grin. She led them into the sitting-room.

Mandy noticed that everywhere was sparklingly clean and smelled pleasantly of lemon-scented polish. Miss Marjorie sat on the sofa with Skye on one side and Jason on the other. She was reading them a story. Miss Joan stood behind her looking over her shoulder.

'We've come to invite you all to Animal Ark on Tuesday to watch the first *Wildlife Ways* TV programme,' Mandy declared. 'You will come, won't you?'

Miss Joan put her hand to her mouth. 'Oh, we don't usually go out, *especially* in the dark!'

'Then perhaps it's time we did,' Miss Marjorie suggested. 'I should love to come, Mandy.'

'We'll take you in the van,' Rowan informed them, dusting the china cabinet. 'If you don't mind a bit of a squeeze.'

'Please come, Miss Joan,' Mandy said. 'There's something in the programme I know you'd love to see.' She winked at James.

'That's true,' James said, joining in. 'You'd be really sorry to miss out.'

'What's up, love?' said Adam Hope, putting an arm round Mandy who was standing outside the back door. She spun around and flung her arms round his waist.

'Oh Dad, I'm *so* nervous,' Mandy said in a shaky voice. 'I've been so excited for the last few days, dying to see the film, and now all of a sudden it's hit me.'

'I'm not surprised, Mandy. After all, it's not every day you're on television,' Adam Hope said. He gently prised her away. 'Come on, you'll be fine. Now if we don't go back in we'll miss it completely.'

Mandy went back into the sitting-room which was crammed with familiar faces. Mandy and James had ended up inviting a *few* more people than Emily Hope had expected, but she'd been great about it and had even laid on refreshments.

Mandy hurried over to her seat as the announcer said, 'And now, *Wildlife Ways*.'

Mandy watched in a trance as Michelle gave her introduction and a picture of the cubs came on. When she saw the cubs' real mother, playing with her cubs and the younger vixen, she couldn't help feeling a lump in her throat. She looked over at James who looked equally upset.

Michelle began her voice-over as the vixen was shown returning with the chicken. She explained how the death of this fox had brought almost the whole of one village together and that because of it, for the meantime, there would be no more foxhunting in the area. When the film cut to the helper vixen hunting and playing with her surrogate cubs, Michelle told the viewers how worried they had all been about her. Then, as the scene changed to the family plus Lucky and his mum, Michelle explained how in the nick of time help had arrived in the form of the young vixen's grandmother. Suddenly, with a jolt, Mandy realised her face was filling the screen and it was her own voice talking. Eventually the camera pulled back and the picture showed Lucky and his mother nuzzling each other and playing with the cubs. There were a few shorter articles and announcements, and then the music started and the credits began to roll.

When the words *Chief Researchers: Mandy Hope and James Hunter* appeared, Mandy's heart skipped a beat. Everyone had stood up and was cheering. She looked over at James, who was blushing, and then around the room. Old Ernie Bell, who had helped them look after Lucky, was beaming, his eyes shining. The Spry sisters were dabbing at their eyes with lace-edged handkerchiefs. And Jason and Skye were talking excitedly, nineteen to the dozen.

'We shall have to get a television, Joan,' Miss Marjorie was saying. 'I insist.'

'Oh, I agree,' Miss Joan said. 'We must certainly purchase one. But how does one go about it?'

'I'm sure Jude and Rowan will help you,' Emily Hope said.

'First thing tomorrow,' Jude agreed.

'You did a grand job there, young Mandy,' Walter Pickard said, coming over to stand beside Mandy. 'And you, young James. And I'm pleased to say you couldn't tell nowt about where it were filmed. So no one's going to go meddling with them foxes.'

Suddenly the phone rang. Simon was nearest and picked it up. 'Mandy, it's for you,' he yelled over the hubbub of chatter and laughter.

Mandy squeezed her way through the crush. 'Hello?' She could hardly hear over the noise.

'Oh, Michelle,' Mandy said into the phone. 'Yes, everybody *loved* it.' She listened for a moment. 'What? Say that again,' she shouted down the phone.

Adam Hope was watching from the other side of the room and he clapped his hands for silence.

'The producers loved the programme,' Mandy relayed to the room, 'and they want Michelle to do a weekly series.' Everybody cheered. She paused, listening and then went on. 'And she says how do we feel about helping with some more research?' Mandy grinned at James who was nodding his head vigorously.

'Great, Michelle,' Mandy said into the phone. 'We'd absolutely love to!'

'Is this all for me?' asked Mandy Hope's father, Adam, as he eyed the large bowl of trifle in front of him.

'No, it is not!' laughed Mandy. 'You're supposed to serve it out to everybody.' She nodded round the kitchen table where her family and friends were gathered for Saturday lunch at Animal Ark.

Mandy had been looking forward to this special lunch with friends and family all together. Adam and Emily Hope, Mandy's parents, had finished morning surgery, and Simon, their assistant, had stayed to lunch along with Grandma and Grandad Hope, Mandy's best friend James Hunter, and their special guest, Michelle Holmes. Michelle was the presenter of the popular radio series, *Wildlife Ways*, which had recently been made into a television programme too.

'Trifle for you, Michelle?' Adam Hope asked, picking up a serving spoon. 'Made by Mandy's own fair hand, you know!'

'Dad!' said Mandy. 'Michelle will think I never cook anything!'

'Yes, please,' Michelle grinned. 'It looks wonderful, Mandy.'

'It looks almost too good to eat,' declared her father, spoon poised over the trifle. 'Here goes . . .' But before he could plunge the spoon into the creamy top the door-bell rang.

'Who can that be at two o'clock on a Saturday afternoon?' Adam Hope groaned.

'Go and see, will you, Mandy?' said Mandy's mum.

'And tell them we're busy,' commanded her father, laughing.

Mandy jumped up from her seat and opened the back door to find Walter Pickard standing there.

'Hi, Mr Pickard. Can I help?' asked Mandy.

'Hello, young Mandy. I wanted a quick word

with your dad,' the elderly man replied.

Mandy hesitated. 'Ah, well, you see we've got guests . . .'

'Oh, I am sorry,' Mr Pickard said, looking embarrassed. 'I didn't mean to interrupt . . . It's just that I've found summat a bit odd . . .'

'Well, you'd better come in.' Mandy held open the door. 'It's Mr Pickard,' she called to the others. 'He's got something to tell you, Dad.' Everyone looked up and smiled a welcome at the elderly man.

'Hello, Walter,' said Adam Hope. 'Come on in.'

But Walter stood near the door, still uncomfortable at the sight of them all sitting down to lunch. 'I'm sorry to disturb you, Mr Hope,' he began.

'Not at all, Walter,' said Mandy's mum. 'Come and sit down. Get that spare chair from the corner for him, Mandy.'

'Yes, come and sit by me,' said Mandy's grandad. 'You look as if you could do with a bit of a rest.'

'Aye, well, I've just been up in Piper's Wood,' Walter explained, pulling up a chair. 'You know the place where Landmere Lane runs between the wood and that old quarry?'

Mandy nodded. 'So what was this odd thing you saw?' she prompted him.

'It weren't so much a *thing* as an *animal*.' Walter looked over at Adam Hope. 'See, first off I thought it were all right . . .' His voice faltered.

'What was it?' Adam Hope prompted.

'Badger. Big young male, he was, in a right mess, an' all . . .' Walter sat down heavily, and frowned, as if trying to puzzle something out.

'Oh, poor thing!' said Mandy.

'What was the trouble with it?' asked her dad.

Walter Pickard shook his head. 'I reckon he were dead,' he said.

'Dead?' Mandy echoed, horrified. 'But how?'

Walter shrugged. 'Looked like summat had had a go at him,' he said. A murmur went round the table.

'Any idea what did it, Walter?' asked Grandad Hope.

He shook his head.

'Perhaps some really fierce animal,' James suggested. He and Mandy both knew that most wild animals would fight an enemy to the death. Walter shook his head. 'There's not many animals 'ud tackle a full-grown badger,' he observed.

Adam Hope nodded. 'I can't think of anything big or brave enough up in the woods around here,' he said. 'Can you, Michelle?'

Michelle thought for a moment. 'Not unless he got in a fight with a really fierce dog,' she suggested. Mandy shivered, remembering the time she and James had rescued an abandoned badger cub from a dug-out sett – in Piper's Wood, too!

'I'd better ring Ted Forrester,' Adam Hope said. Ted was the wildlife inspector at the local RSPCA unit and would want to know about the death of a protected animal.

'He'll need to go up there and collect the body anyway,' Simon observed.

Adam glanced round at the table, where everyone was now busy discussing the news. 'It'll be quieter in the office,' he smiled, and went off to phone Ted.

Mandy's mum sighed. 'We'd better wait and see what's happening before we start on the trifle,' she said. 'You know what Adam's like once he's on a case.'

Mandy smiled at her mother, knowing what she meant: her father was fascinated by wild creatures. If Ted Forrester needed any help investigating the dead badger, Dad would be off to Piper's Wood – guests or no guests!

'See, I wouldn't even touch the poor creature,' Walter was explaining to Grandma Hope, 'in case it were carrying a nasty disease. I've got my three cats to think of.'

Dorothy Hope nodded sympathetically. 'I know how you feel,' she said. 'I wouldn't want to risk my Smoky catching anything either.'

'So that's why I just covered that badger up with leaves and left it there. I knew Mr Hope 'ud know what to do about it,' Walter told her.

Mandy wished with all her heart that Ted Forrester would find the badger still alive. Even if it was badly wounded her father might be able to help it.

Just then, her father came back into the room. 'I'm meeting Ted Forrester in Piper's Wood in about quarter of an hour,' he announced. There was a cry of dismay from the rest of the party.

'I'll come with you,' said Michelle.

Simon nodded. 'Me too!' he said.

'But what about the trifle?' Grandma Hope protested. 'Mandy spent so much time making it . . .'

'We'll have some when we get back,' Adam told her. 'You carry on – we shouldn't be long.

Now, Walter, can you tell me exactly where you left the badger?'

Walter did so, at great length, while Simon got his emergency bag and Michelle fetched her jacket.

Mandy looked across at James, who nodded slightly. 'Take James and me with you, Dad, *please*,' she begged.

Mr Hope thought for a moment and then nodded. 'But we've got to get off right away – no messing about!' he warned.

Mandy and James were already rushing out to the Land-rover.

'We'll stay and clear this lot up,' said Grandma Hope, looking at the remains of the lunch party. 'We can have the trifle with tea when you all get back. You'll stay too, won't you, Walter?' she asked kindly.

Walter Pickard beamed. 'So long as you let me help you with all this clearing up. I'm a good little washer-upper!'

The others piled into the Land-rover and were soon off down the lane and through the village. They didn't say much; the party spirit had quite evaporated with the news of the dead badger.

'At least we got out of the washing-up,' Mr Hope said, trying to jolly them along a bit. But

Mandy couldn't laugh. She was wondering just what they would find when they arrived at the other end of Piper's Wood.

Mr Hope drove up to Landmere Lane, round the far side of the woods. When he turned off the lane they scraped and bumped their way up the rough forestry track until it became so narrow even the Land-rover could go no further.

'Everybody out!' he announced, pulling up.

They all piled out and stood looking into the wood.

'No sign of Ted Forrester yet,' observed Simon.

'He'll be along soon,' said Adam Hope, coming round to join them. 'Meanwhile, we can be looking for a silver-birch copse – that's where Walter said he'd seen the dead badger. Ted will find us when he gets here.'

The others all piled out and looked around. Piper's Wood was an old, mixed forest, with oaks and elms and beeches interspersed with younger silver birches. Adam led the way, pushing through the brambles which almost covered the path, and Mandy followed close behind.

'How on earth did Mr Pickard get through this lot?' James muttered.

'He didn't,' said Mandy. 'He was walking down from the top of the woods, remember. There's a bridle-path over there.'

Soon they pushed their way into a clearing in the birch woods, just as Walter had described, and the others caught up with them.

'Now, all we need to do is find the place Walter hid the badger!' said Mr Hope, surveying the scene.

Mandy followed his gaze anxiously. She was still half hoping they'd find the badger alive. If they found it in time maybe her dad could save it.

'Go carefully, just in case the animal isn't dead,' Simon warned, as they began their search.

Mandy's spirits rose. Just hearing Simon admit there was a chance of helping the poor badger made her feel better. She set off, determined to be the one who found him. They walked slowly and cautiously through the grasses and bracken, heads bent, eyes on the ground.

It was Michelle who called out, 'I think I've found him!' She prodded a heap of leaves with the toe of her boot.

They ran across to help her and soon they

were standing looking down at the sleek, grey-black body of a large, full-grown male badger. At first glimpse he appeared to be streaked with dirt and mud, but as Mandy looked more closely she saw it was blood that was staining his brindled grey coat. 'Oh, the poor, poor thing!' she whispered.

Simon crouched down beside Adam Hope and asked him something in a low voice. Mandy saw her father shake his head, sadly. 'There's no pulse,' he said simply.

The badger was dead all right. Mandy turned and blinked away the tears. Michelle came over and put an arm around her and gave her a little hug.

'I know it's hard, Mandy,' she said, softly. 'Working with wild animals always is, you know that.' Mandy nodded and sniffed hard.

'And it doesn't get any easier, either,' Michelle said. 'I'll always hate facing up to seeing a dead animal.'

'What do you think happened to him, Dad?' Mandy asked, brushing away a tear.

Her father pulled on a pair of rubber gloves and, kneeling by the body, began to examine it carefully. 'I can see the cuts and scratches now,' he said. 'And some deep bites round his neck.'

'So do you think he could have been fighting?' asked Michelle.

Mandy shuddered. 'Fighting with dogs, you mean?'

Michelle nodded. They all knew that badger-baiting was a 'sport' that had come to Welford once before. Perhaps it was all happening again!

'Not necessarily,' her father replied. Then he sighed. 'But it *is* a possibility.'

They stood there in silence, watching Simon clear the rest of the leaves off the badger. Mandy looked over at James and saw he was frowning.

'Are you thinking what I'm thinking?' he said.

'Bonser?' Mandy murmured. James nodded unhappily. Mr Bonser had been prosecuted for organising badger-baiting in Welford once before – mainly on evidence that Mandy and James had collected.

'Don't go jumping to conclusions!' Mandy's dad warned. 'Badgers have other enemies besides men and their dogs.'

'Bonser left the district after he was prosecuted, didn't he?' said James.

Mandy sighed, thinking about Mr Bonser. What if he had come back? What if this dead badger had something to do with him? Mandy felt herself going cold all over.

Suddenly they heard the sound of a car lurching up the track. A door slammed, and someone moved cautiously through the under-growth and worked their way along the bridle-path on the other side of the clearing. Mandy stiffened and looked across the clearing, hardly daring to breathe. Was this one of the badger baiters, she wondered, come back to bury the evidence? Could it be Mr Bonser himself?